Ten Yen Tokyo
The Miracle Continues

Christina St. Clair
Amanda Armstrong

Published by Rogue Phoenix Press
Copyright © 2016

978-1-62420-273-5

Credits
Cover Artist: Designs by Ms G
Editor: Christie L. Kraemer

Dedication

For mothers everywhere…

"…and for my beautiful daughter, Mia, who has made the most important job I've ever had, the easiest." Amanda Armstrong

"…and for, Lily, my mum who didn't want a daughter but loved me in spite of all the difficulties of raising babies in post WW II London." Christina St Clair

Prologue

I can't believe I'm doing this. What kind of person am I? Leaving my own baby behind and him not yet two weeks old. It's not that I'm leaving him in a basket by the river, or putting him in a fire truck and turning on the alarm to alert the firemen. I am leaving him with a caring father who is gaga over him and four grandparents who think he is the most precious baby they have ever seen. My mom and dad act as if he's the reincarnation of the baby boy they lost.

Mom keeps hugging him and saying, "You are so precious, so perfect," in a hushed voice. It makes me wonder if she thought I was going to birth a kid with the sort of severe birth defects *her* baby had. My brother. He only lived a few hours after birth. I've not said a word to Mom about how I was almost twenty years younger than she when she had Stephen and how her age might have been part of the reason for his pitiful physical condition. I admit, though, during my pregnancy, I did have a few pangs of fear and was glad when the amniocentesis was okay. Lucas is thriving and healthy.

I simply cannot become gaga over him. When I said I didn't want him during the pregnancy, everyone ignored me or patted my back and told me not to worry. As soon as I saw him and held him against my breast, they said I'd fall in love. But I knew I wouldn't. And I didn't. I wanted a girl. In fact I want four baby girls who will love to dance and sing, who will straighten one another's hair, who will giggle at night after I turn the lights out. But now I'll not have any more babies, because what man will want to bond with me if he finds out I abandoned my first child. And I want honesty in my relationship. I don't want secrets between my man and me.

I could, I suppose, change my name. But how will I manage that?

Unless I really am the person behind the name, it will be a big lie. I need to travel far away. I think I will go to the west coast, maybe to Seattle. I could get lost in a big city easily enough where no one will ever find me. I can keep my name and social security number and get a job.

Will John try to find me? Perhaps he'll send the police after me. They might locate me. I'll have to leave a note telling John I have left. Forever. Explaining my love for John wasn't enough, and I have no love at all for this baby boy. I told John to name him whatever he likes—he wanted me to choose, but I didn't care enough. I could not come up with one single name—which is a sure sign of the depth of my feeling of, well, disinterest. I am not interested in caring for this infant. He should have been a girl and things might have been different.

How will I cope without my parents? They will be so hurt, so worried, but they have my twin sister. She is not identical but she is much more pleasant than I've ever been. A bit controlling maybe, but usually no trouble. Me, I was always a rebel, always giving mom and dad grief. I could change my name from the awful one they stuck with me that gave me nothing but misery growing up. *Seagull*. Can you imagine being called such a thing! I hated it as a child when other kids would raise their arms like wings.

But now, I see, it was right for me. I am Seagull. I am about to fly.

Oh yeah, my twin sister's name is Sarah. Of course. She will, like the Biblical Sarah, have a baby she adores when she's in her nineties. I suspect she may have quite a few sooner since she just married Doug who is her dream guy. Okay, he's not an athlete, but she loves him for his geeky glasses, his sweet smile, his puny arms.

My John is so macho, so masculine. He matches me.

But I must fly. I *must* fly.

~ * ~

I've been standing here on this bridge for almost three hours now. My gaze keeps being drawn to the water some way beneath. I know if I make the jump, I will die, but a part of me also wonders if just like my name, my spirit will fly and soar.

I won't jump though. I have too much life within me to end it now. It cannot and will not be governed by the baby boy who invaded my body and the man who once claimed my body as his.

No, I need to get away and it needs to be somewhere far, where they can't find me.

Suddenly it hits me. If they thought I was dead, they wouldn't attempt to look for me.

I could start afresh without ever having to look over my shoulder and could concentrate on making the most of my future.

I untie the silk scarf from around my neck. It's a navy blue one with little pink birds on it. John gave it to me the day after we discovered I was pregnant. I've always hated it, but I pretended to love it. I am sick of compromises to give everyone else what they need. Why didn't I smile and thank John for his gift then exchange it for something I really liked? Why didn't John know I do not like long flowing silk scarves, especially ones with birds on them. Pink birds. I have always despised pink, and he knows I don't like my bird name. I suppose he hoped to change me into his version of a pretty girl in pink who adores infants.

I'm a doctor, for Christ's sake. I can imagine being in the ER bending over someone bleeding from a gunshot wound, and the end of the scarf acting like a wick sucking up blood, or even worse, contaminating the patient. Fuck, John, what were you thinking? But what was I thinking to keep on wearing it day-in and day-out? It has been a constant reminder of the ache in my heart and the confusion in my mind about having a baby boy.

I hold it out above the river. With a grim smile on my face, I watch as it drops from my hand and glides over the bridge, into the water.

One: John

John knew from the moment he entered the house she was gone. The old wireless that would usually be throbbing with Seagull's favorite pop music sat ominously silent. Missing too was her scent in the air, a musky coconut perfume fragrance he adored.

Little Lucas was sleeping in his crib. When he reached down and felt his infant son's dry diaper, he knew she couldn't have been gone for too long. She must have changed him before she left. Besides, he'd only been out a short time to pick up bread and milk from the store.

He walked quietly up to their bedroom, his heart beating way too fast, not knowing what he might find, half-expecting her to be in there naked, smiling at him, welcoming him, but she'd been weird during her pregnancy and had gotten even more distant after the baby came. She wouldn't even discuss names with him. He'd known something was wrong. He knew something was wrong now too. Inside the bedroom, the bed, as usual, was made, by him. It looked too neat, too orderly. He opened the closet, relieved to see all of her jeans, long-sleeved tee-shirts, and her two dresses, both black, crushed against her hospital scrubs.

He held his panic inside. He knew she'd been depressed, but many moms went through post-partum depression. She'd even discussed it with him, being the ever so clinical doctor as if *he* were the patient, as if they weren't talking about *her* behavior. He'd done his best to be understanding, promised she'd feel better, while planning to secretly talk to her obstetrician. Even if she hadn't been herself lately, who would leave their newborn child? Maybe she *had* dashed out for more diapers? Except she'd have called him to tell him to get them, wouldn't she? In the past when he was on an errand, she often called him to remind him to get something.

He went back downstairs through the living room, peeking in once again at Lucas who was still sleeping peacefully. Their little kitchen felt silent and empty. Sea never liked this house, always said she found it too small and suffocating. She loved space, loved being outside. He'd planned, when he began to sell books, to buy her a house with a big yard, maybe even out in the country. Of course, it would take a best-seller, and so far he'd not gotten so much as a polite rejection for the many submissions he'd made to all the big publishers. Sea always supported him, telling him to hang onto his dreams and not give up. He'd wondered at times if in reality she felt disappointed. She should have damn well said so!

Before Lucas, he would often return home from work to find her sitting on the front lawn, barefooted, making daisy chains. Or she would be dancing wildly through the little garden sprinkler, much to the disdain of some of their more conservative neighbors. Seagull didn't care though. Not then. She was always a free little bird. It's one of the reasons he'd fallen in love with her.

Right from the first day he met her on campus.

Her laugh had caught his attention. She'd thrown her head back and let it out, a shameless burst of uninhibited joy. Her passionate nature inspired him. He wished then and still did that he was such a free spirit.

He'd finally approached her at one of the frat parties she often went to. Life and soul, she'd been drinking straight from a bottle of Jack and swaying gently to the music. Her light brown hair worn long back then, fell down her back almost to her waist. Her porcelain skin, slightly tanned from a recent sunny spell was glazed with the sheen of perspiration.

"I'm John." He'd introduced himself.

She'd turned her gaze to him, looking him up and down with those knowing green eyes and a not unkind half-grin on her face.

"John the jock?" she'd stated with a twinkle in her eyes before letting that laughter take over again. He couldn't help joining in.

From then on, they were inseparable. He was besotted with her. He had to admit he still was actually.

Where was she?

From the crib in the living room, he heard Lucas stirring. In moments,

John rushed to the baby's side and gently scooped him out of the crib, holding him to his shoulder, breathing in his wonderful baby scent. "Hush, little man," he whispered. "Daddy's here." He glanced over to the little carriage clock on the mantelpiece and decided to give it another hour before he started making any calls.

Two: Seagull

Seagull had a moment of doubt when she looked into the baby's crib and she *did* grab a few photos from an album. She wanted to take the big-framed one of mom and dad, Sarah and her when they were at Myrtle Beach. It had been such a great family time, but John would notice it missing. For sure he'd never in a million years look in her old photo album though. It wouldn't interest him, buried beneath a mound of other old scrapbooks, including the one with pictures of Cumberland Falls in Kentucky where they went for their honeymoon. She did *not* look in it. She refused to get nostalgic. It was totally, totally freeing to leave everything behind.

Yet here she was driving her rental car in Kentucky, knowing full well she couldn't be too far from Cumberland Falls, yearning for those carefree days when their love-making was explosive. She was tempted to drive over there to take a look. John used to seem such a hunk, so masculine, so steady too, and such a creative guy, tender and macho. She wanted that John back, but he'd gotten sloppy sentimental over having a kid, and their love-making dwindled. She'd tried to entice him, but once pregnant, she'd had no interest in sex at all.

Her memories overwhelmed her. They'd been so in love, but that went out the window along with her expectations of pretty daughters to go shopping with, and dress up, and teach to sing and dance. He'd been thrilled they were having a boy, a son to carry on the name. She'd hated that tradition, hated that she'd taken his name and not kept her own. It was all too doggone late.

In spite of her confused emotions, she wondered if her strong desire for daughters arose out of her childhood, her *happy* childhood, before her mother lost it. Was it possible, Seagull pondered, her disinterest in her infant son related to that time when mom started a journey in and out of mental institutions after losing her baby son? Seagull was fifteen when it began. But she was *not* depressed like that, and she'd told John when she'd discussed with him the symptoms of post-partum depression that wasn't her problem. She was not lying in bed day and night hardly able to open her eyes. Sad as she now felt, it was a result of leaving. It was *always* sad to leave someone behind. Breaking up was hard to do. Furthermore, by leaving, her hope was restored. She wasn't wishing the kid dead. She simply didn't want to be a mother.

Her plan was to turn in the rental car at Louisville Airport and fly to the West Coast. She patted a grocery bag on the passenger seat. It was one of those skimpy ones from Walmart. It bulged with the money she'd secretly squirreled away from her job at Allegheny General Hospital. She couldn't help her grin at having double-bagged it. She felt practical and clever, skilled, remembering her exciting days in the emergency room, where in spite of the constant demands of night call and trauma, she'd thrived. Sure, she'd crabbed to John about how difficult her job was, and she wouldn't miss the stress, would she? He'd insisted she quit. At the time, she'd gone meekly along with him, wanting the best for the unborn kid, but now she realized she would miss those adrenalin rushes when she'd had to intubate patients and staunch open wounds. John wanted her to start a practice out in the country. She did love the open fields near Pittsburgh and knew John only meant to make her happy. How could a man be so out of tune with his wife?

Perhaps she'd go to Seattle and apply for a surgical internship. Why not? She could do it. Her hopes rose at undreamed-of possibilities ahead of her now that she was free. Her mind continued to wander, dreaming of the future, but she needed to pay attention to the big green road signs. They were everywhere, indicating left and right turns onto the various Interstates. She started getting panicky about which lane to get into. Would she need to make a left or a right? Damn, she wished she had her GPS.

At last, she glimpsed the overhead sign to Louisville indicating the far right lane. Damn, sandwiched between two semis, she couldn't see. Further damn. Her lane ended and there was way too much traffic. She slammed down the accelerator, planning to speed in front of the truck, and that's when she spun out of control.

She remembered hitting the guard rail.

Next thing, she was in an emergency room on a gurney with white-coated doctors and nurses and medical staff all around. She heard the word *trauma. What the fuck?* She was the one supposed to be rendering life-giving care, not receiving it. Besides, she was okay. Her head felt a bit sore but other than that, she was sure she was okay. She tried to get up.

"Whoa," a big black guy told her, gently taking her shoulders. "You stay still until we get you an MRI to make sure you don't have a head injury. You wrecked your car, so I heard. It's a miracle you survived with just a few cuts and abrasions."

He had kind eyes. But Seagull worried once they had her identity, they would try to call next of kin. She hadn't cleaned out her wallet, and her social security card was in there, along with her driver's license and credit cards. "I'm okay," she said.

Suddenly remembering her bag of money, she tried to swing her legs off the side of the stretcher. "Where's my stuff?"

"Don't you worry," the black guy, probably a nurse, told her. "Your possessions will be gotten to you once we've got you fixed up."

There wasn't a damn thing she could do but hope for the best and go along with their program. If she tried to leave, she'd only bring more attention to herself, and with any luck, she would get back her credit cards and her money. She felt herself begin to perspire.

Next thing she knew she'd been admitted to a room with an IV dripped into her vein and all the usual monitors hooked up; blood pressure, heart rate, respirations.

In spite of feelings of dread, she dozed off.

"Seagull," the voice of a white-coated lady woke her. "I'm Doctor Buchanan," she said. "MRI showed no brain bleeds. You've got a mild concussion. Other than that, you are in good condition. We want you to stay overnight for observation, then you'll be free to go."

Seagull looked into the eyes of the doctor and was reminded of herself, slight in build with a professional smile plastered onto her face.

"Who do you want us to contact?"

"No one," Seagull mumbled. "I have no one. I was on my way to the airport."

"Okay," the doctor said, and patted Seagull's hand. "Rest, watch TV. You'll be out of here and on your way before long. Someone will give you back your effects and clothes—they are a bit messy. Your car was towed, by the way. I'll have a social worker look in on you and arrange for you to carry on with your journey."

Three: Seagull

A radio in the nurse's station announced it was eight in the morning when Seagull awoke in the hospital room. It made her cringe to be the patient and not the one in charge, but it also made her more sympathetic to the plight of trauma victims. As an ER physician, she'd been all business. Now she'd gotten an inside taste of how it felt to be an accident casualty and even if she didn't have anything more than a few bruises and no serious head-injuries, it still felt horrible. She felt as if she'd been battered and thrown out of a speeding truck. But she knew she had to be strong and get a move on because she was about to be released.

But released to what? Her resolve to leave John and her family and never go back felt a little shakier than it had before. She wanted to cry. Her breasts were aching and she was sweating.

She willed herself on. *Damn, damn, damn. I am going to fly. My name isn't Seagull for nothing.*

That stupid car accident hadn't been her fault except she remembered very little of what had happened. She knew it was common for trauma cases to experience memory loss, so she wasn't terribly worried.

But, she thought, what if it's a sign? *A sign that the accident about to happen in my life is me.*

She remembered how horrible it was taking care of her dad after her little brother died. Not to mention having to bathe her mom. It went on for months before her mother began to regain strength and vitality. Her dad had been so damn needy too. She'd hated that she and her sister Sarah had to cook and clean for them.

Seagull's high school years were a blur of confusion. She'd expected to be prom queen and be able to hang out with boys, drive fast cars, and smoke dope, but instead she'd been coaxing her mother to live.

Perhaps that's why her college years had seen her going a bit off the rails. Well, until she'd met John anyway.

But now, she refused to allow these thoughts to overwhelm her. She felt as if she needed a sedative, not the coffee she'd just drunk, weak though it was. The social worker had brought it to her when she'd given her back her wallet, purse and a pair of jeans with a plaid shirt she'd got from a charity shop. Seagull appreciated the clean underwear, even though baggy cotton panties were not exactly her style. It was better than nothing fresh. Luckily, she'd found jeans and a shirt that fit. They made her feel like a cowgirl. The social worker was a nice lady, though, and she certainly didn't want to complain.

Now, she was supposed to wait for a doctor to officially sign her release papers, but she was heading out of here immediately. Her cell phone was in her purse, and she intended to call the car rental place to send her another car. Hopefully, they would. Back home they would, but this was Kentucky. She had no idea if car rental companies were the same everywhere. She felt so jittery, but she couldn't think this way. *I am so doggone paranoid*, she thought, but more scary thoughts took over her mind. *What if I have no money? What if someone stole it while I was unconscious?* Seagull frantically searched the pile of clothes and found the Walmart bag on the bed. Her money was all there. Thank God. She felt slightly more confident.

But the moment she crept out into the hallway, she froze. A cop was heading her way. She ducked back into the hospital room, her heart pounding like a jackhammer, hoping the uniformed guy hadn't seen her, but knowing he had, hoping he wasn't coming for her. His footsteps stopped outside her room and he peered in. He was tall and broad, striking in his dark jacket with the black shoulder stripes. His face was serious and his eyes concerned. She couldn't believe her response, but she felt, well, sensual. *Jesus, Seagull, calm down. You are being so weird.*

"Ma'am," the officer said. "I'm Trooper Johnson. You're Seagull, correct?"

She caught the tiny grin on his face when he said Seagull and wished she had put on makeup. "Yes, that's me," she said, trying not to tremble, not to show her attraction to this guy. What was wrong with her?

"I'm the officer who filed the accident report at the scene. I'm glad to see you're okay. I was passing the hospital on my way to the station and decided to check on you. Is your husband coming to fetch you?"

"Husband," she muttered, noticing the white circle of skin on her ring finger where she'd removed her wedding band. He must have seen it. She blurted out, "My marriage is over. I'm on my way to a new job, a new life!" *What am I saying? Shut up,* she told herself. *Shut up!* "Am I in trouble? Was anyone else hurt?"

"No, Ma'am, on both counts. Trucker reported you hit an oily patch in the road and your car spun out of control. We notified the car rental company. They will probably be in touch with you, but your insurance and driver's license were all in order."

Seagull's relief that he wasn't there to send her home or take her to jail was totally deflating. She sank onto the bed. "Thank God," she managed to whisper.

Although the officer's mouth remained stern, his eyes softened. "I'm sorry to hear about your troubles. I'm divorced myself. It took a while for me to get back on my feet. I thought I'd never want or find another wife, but life happens. I've been happily remarried for five years." He took out his cell phone and showed her a picture of a pretty smiling girl holding a baby.

Seagull almost choked but managed to smile and mutter, "They are beautiful. You must be very proud." She prayed he wouldn't start telling her about his baby.

"Don't you worry," he said. "You'll be okay. You take care now." He turned to go but stopped near the bedside locker. "Don't forget these coins," he said, picking up some change and gazing at it curiously.

Seagull's hand involuntarily rose into the air with her fingers outstretched towards him. He dropped one copper coin then three more into her palm. They clicked together and Seagull stared at them.

The officer continued to peer at the coins. "What are they? Chinese?"

"Japanese," Seagull replied. She wasn't sure how she knew, but she was filled with a strange sense of certainty in spite of her sweaty armpits.

Four: Seagull

As Seagull raced towards the exit, desperate to get the hell out of the hospital, she ran straight into a young woman. The coins flew out of her hand and spilled onto the floor. "Sorry, sorry," she mumbled, hastily dropping to her knees, trying to hang onto her bag of money and her purse while scrabbling up the coins.

"Hey, it's ok, let me help." The woman's accent wasn't from around these parts.

"Thanks." Seagull shrugged, keeping her head bent as the woman crouched beside her, not wanting her to see her face. *Jeez, I have to get out of here. Thank Christ the car-rental place brought me a car so fast.*

"Hey, these coins! Where did you get them?" The woman, who Seagull now realized was British, suddenly became animated. Seagull quickly grabbed the last coin off the ground before the woman could take it.

"Where did you get them?" the British woman repeated, and her voice raised an octave.

What the hell is it to do with her?

"A friend…" Seagull stood up, ready to run if the lady questioned her further, but she had simply touched her arm, waiting for Seagull to look at her.

Seagull glanced up at her through her bangs and raised an eyebrow.

The woman shook her head and removed her hand from Seagull who straightened up and turned to go.

"Good luck," the woman called out softly, but Seagull didn't look back. She had no idea who she was and didn't care much either, but something about her touch had felt familiar, and that scared the shit out of

14

her. She finally reached the parking lot and located her rental, breathing a sigh of relief as she unlocked the driver's door.

Sticking the clutch into reverse, she looked in her rear view mirror and gasped as a chill ran through her. The young British woman was standing at the entrance to the hospital, staring right at her car. Her face was familiar, not just from their chance collision, but Seagull couldn't place her. *Shit, is it somebody I know? Has my mind blanked her out? Maybe I have a worse concussion than I realized. Jesus, I hope I can function.* She managed to quickly back the car out and burn rubber on the way out of the parking lot, leaving the hospital and *that* woman behind.

This was not good. Her aim was to leave with nobody seeing her. The only trace of her was to be her clothes in the river, back in Pennsylvania. That was stage one and now she had to think about stage two, where exactly to go. As she squirmed in her seat to get comfortable for the drive, she felt something dig into her hip through her pants. Keeping one hand on the wheel, she arched her back to pull the coins out of her front pocket and threw them in the coin tray beside her.

She hadn't considered yet as to how they came to be on her locker, nor how she had known they were Japanese. It was too weird. She'd think about that later. For now, she had to keep on driving.

Suddenly, she saw a huge billboard with the face of *that* British woman smiling at her. She almost spun out of control. Again. But she quickly read the large headline: Caitlin Morgan-Sommerville, Norton Director of Marketing, Welcomes You to National Hospital Week. There was a date and more information, but she was already flying down the highway and couldn't read it.

She'd intended on going directly to Louisville Airport, leaving the car there, and getting the next plane to the West Coast, but her head began to throb. She needed food, and she needed rest. She hadn't slept well in the hospital room, and the scare with the cop had stressed her. As if she wasn't stressed enough.

Seagull could see Louisville skyscrapers and took the first ramp into the city to find a hotel. She decided to stay at the Brown in the downtown section. It looked posh, but she could care less about money. *I can surely afford one night. I still have a credit card I can use. It's in my name, so John won't get the bill. John!* She didn't want to think about how he might be feeling. Worried. Frantic. Emotional. He'd probably not stopped crying. He was always way too sentimental, boo-hooing over silly movies.

She got a room and fortunately didn't have to wait till the afternoon. It was spacious with two queen beds, a small fridge, a desk and a flat-screen TV. Seagull ordered bacon and eggs and biscuits from room service—heart-clogging food she'd never touch back home. But she was making a new home, and what did she care if her heart stopped? This thought gave her pause. *I do care. My heart was stopped, at least figuratively, immobile, passive, lying low from everyone else telling me how to be a good mom. I am leaving, changing, to find my heart again.* It had nothing to do with food. If she wanted a good greasy breakfast, she'd have one. At least for today. Tomorrow maybe she'd eat oatmeal and yogurt.

The bacon was crispy. The eggs were done just right, scrambled with milk and butter, and the biscuits which she slathered with honey were delicious. Leaving the rich coffee, afraid it would make her headache worse, Seagull managed to doze off with the TV on.

When she opened her eyes it was to see the British chick again, Caitlin something or other, on the local TV news. She'd acted really weird about those coins the cop had given her—but maybe, Seagull suddenly realized, maybe they belonged to her. It was an odd thing, she could leave an infant and husband and family forever, but felt like a criminal for stealing someone else's money. The woman had said good luck in a strange voice too. What had that been about? There was no way she could possibly have guessed what Seagull was doing—escaping.

Damn, you'd think she'd been abused and she hadn't been. Ever. Certainly not by John. And not by her parents either. Not even after her little brother had died. Nor before when they'd been an ideal family, always laughing—unless that was a false memory about a fake family who were never so perfect. But wasn't she entitled to her own life? She was tired of fulfilling everyone's expectations. She'd become a doctor because it was what her mom always wanted to do rather than be a nurse. She was about to become her own person, unencumbered and free. She might not even practice medicine again.

John had his freedom. But without her that would change. He'd no longer be able to stay home as much to write his novel, because there wouldn't be her paycheck covering the mortgage. He might have to get a better job. He'd have to hire a babysitter, but his mom would probably be glad to do it. Her mom would too, except she lived too far away. Not her problem anymore.

She decided to wander outside and go to an Internet café. She knew she shouldn't, but she clicked on John's website. *Damn, damn, I need to not go there.* The photo of his smiling face greeted her, and in his arms was the baby in a blue one-piece. It made her cringe. Guilt was an ugly thing. But even worse he'd posted a blog about her having gone missing, a plea for anyone who had seen her to call him or the police. Apparently, he'd tried to get the police to issue an all points bulletin, but it turned out APB's were to locate criminals and not to find missing persons. His blog continued:

Seagull is everything to me. We have a baby together, Lucas. I cannot believe my sweet wife is gone. The police say someone saw a woman who looked like my wife staring at the river. They asked me if she left a suicide note. She didn't. She wouldn't! They suggested she might have left with another guy. I resented their inquisition even though I know they have to ask the questions. Worst of all they found blue jeans and a tee-shirt near the water, folded neatly. I wasn't for sure they belonged to Sea, but then they handed me a silk scarf they said was dangling from a waterlogged tree about a hundred yards downstream. It was the one I gave her after we found out she was expecting Lucas. She loves it. She'd never have taken it off her neck. I am so afraid she's been abducted by some creep. I am begging you to share her photo and story, tweet it, get it out everywhere! I know she's alive. I refuse to believe she's dead. Her baby needs her. I want her home.

Tears trickled down Seagull's face. *I am so sorry, John. I don't want to cause anyone pain, especially not you.* She was tempted to call him, to tell him she was okay but would not be coming back. Ever. But she knew if she heard his voice, he would persuade her to be honorable and take up her parental duties, and she couldn't. She just couldn't. But where could she go if her photo was all over the internet? Someone was bound to recognize her. The photo of her was recent, taken in Riverside Park. She was standing near the aviary, smiling. Her hair would be a giveaway. She was a redhead right now and looked like Amy Adams in American Hustle. She'd have to cut her hair short and dye it.

That's when she remembered the coins she'd left in the car. Japan. She'd go there. But how would she manage to find her way in a country where she didn't speak the language? She didn't even know what visas she might need. But she knew she was going there for sure. Tokyo. *That's it. I am sure I need to go there, and the cherry blossoms will be in bloom. But first I am going to find that Caitlin with the British accent and give her back the coins which must surely be hers.*

Five: Caitlin

Caitlin Morgan-Somerville sat at her desk, gaping at the words she read on her computer screen: "*Missing, Seagull Hudson, possible suicide!*" She enlarged the image of the woman's face attached to the article. Yes, she was sure. It was the woman she'd seen with the coins!

Instinctively she picked up her phone. She needed to let the police know and that poor anxious husband of hers. She pushed nine then one, but as her finger went to press the last number, her office door flew open.

"Hey, baby!"

Caitlin put her phone down with a smile of pleasure for her husband, Paul. "Baby, I've told you not to turn up unannounced here. I'm supposed to be working." Her tone was admonishing, but the warmth she felt inside at the sight of her lovely man was unmistakable.

Paul pulled a sad face. "Want me to go?"

She giggled. "No, no, you're here now." She stood up and walked around her desk to kiss him. "What's up?"

"Thought I'd take you to lunch."

Caitlin glanced at her wrist watch. "It's ten thirty, Paul!"

"Brunch?" Paul raised a questioning eyebrow and Caitlin laughed.

"No, I have things to do. But hey look at this." She took his hand, leading him back to her desk and tapped the screen.

Paul leaned in towards the computer. "Mmm, pretty girl."

Caitlin slapped his arm. "Read it. She's missing."

Paul nodded as he read. "Yeah, pretty sad," he mused. "Anyway, brunch?"

"I saw her, Paul. She was here yesterday."

Paul stood up straight and looked at Caitlin.

"Ok…" He waited for her to continue.

"Well, I should tell the police, shouldn't I?"

Paul narrowed his eyes at her. "What's stopping you?"

Caitlin sighed. "I was actually just about to but…"

Paul waited.

"But, I'm not sure, Paul. There was something about her. And she had the coins!"

Paul groaned. "Goddamn. Not those again!" He sunk into her desk chair and put his head in his hands. "So what do you want to do?" he asked without looking up.

Caitlin stroked his bent head absentmindedly as she gazed once again at Seagull's face on her computer. "I don't know. If I tell the police, it will at least put that poor husband of hers out of his misery."

Paul was nodding. "There you go. There's your answer right there."

Caitlin suddenly crouched in front of him. "But what if she ran away from him because he beats her or something?"

"Cait, you can't assume anything. Just call the police. You have to." Paul's eyes pleaded with hers.

She held his gaze for several seconds before replying. "Not yet, baby," she shook her head, her mind suddenly made up. "I don't know why fate allowed that we should meet, but we did. Plus she had the coins. There's a reason for this."

"Baby…" Paul held her shoulders gently and kissed her forehead. "No more coins. Please?"

"I'm sorry, Paul. I just have a feeling about this."

Six: John

John stared at his computer screen, overwhelmed by the e-mails that kept on popping up faster than he could open them. They were all in response to his cry for help in finding Seagull:

Seen her with another guy.

She's a whore.

I murdered her and threw her body in a drainage ditch.

Trust and the Lord will help you.

Don't give up hope.

Aliens abducted her.

I am going to cut the bitch. She's chained in my cellar. I want to make her scream.

He felt as if he should answer them all, but that last one made him want to throw up. He felt helpless and bewildered and very angry at the hate-filled ones. What made people so mean? So fucking crazy?

He got up and went over to the photo of Seagull, looking professional in her business suit, accepting her medical degree. He'd been so proud of her. What a girl he'd married. He couldn't believe she'd wanted him, accepted him, loved him. But she had. Did! Still did! She used to tell him how macho he was, but he'd always felt inadequate, aware she deserved more than he could offer. He hung his head, feeling deeply ashamed. They'd used artificial insemination for the baby. The very first time had taken.

"Sea, little Sea, where are you," he moaned, and sank onto the bed near his desk, hugging his knees and sobbing. Her body hadn't been found. He'd been convinced putting out her photo on the Internet on his blog would bring her back, but instead he felt as if he'd been run over by a truck. The image chilled him. What if Seagull *was* lying somewhere bleeding, or imprisoned, being raped!

The cries from Lucas made him stir. He wiped away his tears and blew his nose. He went to his son and picked him up, kissing the top of the baby's head. "It's all right, sweet boy, Mommy will come home. I promise."

But he knew he couldn't promise.

After he'd changed Lucas's diaper, given him his bottle and settled him down, he found himself in front of the computer again. His hand scrolled down the list of e-mails, but he didn't want to open any more. Couldn't face them.

Suddenly, the computer screen flashed with an error message, but he didn't have time to read it before his computer crashed. Nothing he did seemed to bring it back to life. His stomach seized up; his heart felt like a marble in his chest. He sat for ten minutes trying to decide what to do next. Should he call his mother, Jane? She had a doctorate and worked at Carnegie Mellon. She was a computer nerd. She'd know how to get back online, assuming the computer had simply been overloaded with incoming junk and didn't have enough RAM. Unless some cruel jackass had sent him a virus.

He wasn't sure he even wanted to get back online to face all those messages, even if some of them were well-meaning. How was he to follow the leads from people swearing they'd seen Sea in Topeka, Kansas when at the same time she'd been spotted hundreds of miles away on the east coast in Philadelphia?

He tapped number two on his cell to automatically dial his mother, Jane's, number. Reluctantly. He'd always protected Sea from Jane's competitive meanness. Sea would never know how Jane had said to him right before they got married, *You are my son, and she* (meaning Sea) *will never be first with you.* She'd systematically and privately continued to bad-mouth Sea to him for the three years they'd been married.

"My darling boy," Jane answered. "Any word?"
"No, Mom. My computer crashed. I need someone to help me get it back online. I'm getting a lot of helpful leads." He didn't know why he lied—perhaps because he hoped there *would* be some helpful leads. It would only take one. Maybe he ought to go to Topeka. What if she *was* there? He could ask the contact to describe her, find a way to screen the responses he was

getting—throw out the crazies and mean ones, and concentrate on helpful kind ones. One thing he was not going to do was feed what he suspected would be Jane's hopes that Sea was gone for good.

Her voice was silken and cool. "I'll leave work immediately. Don't worry, John, I'll fix this."

Within half an hour, she arrived in a flurry. "Lucas okay?" she asked and didn't bother to listen to John's reply but went immediately into the nursery, checked the baby's diaper, removed the tattered sheet which John had put in there because he hoped it smelled of Sea.

"Leave that, Mom," John said. "It probably has Sea's scent."

Jane glared at him. "It's dirty." She tossed it onto a nearby chair and rummaged through a pile of linens, selecting the blanket she'd purchased from an exclusive online baby store. "There you are, Lucas," she cooed in a voice that sounded to John like the squawking of a crow. "Are you giving him enough formula?" she asked.

John hid his exasperation. "Lucas is fine. Please come and look at the computer." *Why oh why did I let her into my house?* He led her into the bedroom they'd converted into his office, where he kept his computer.

Tapping the on and off button and asking him what exactly had happened, she merely nodded. He didn't know why, but he felt like an idiot. She rambled on about various causes of computer crashes. Finally, she said, "It's not a critical kernel. It's overload." With that she crawled under his desk, unplugged everything from the wall and waited a minute or so before plugging everything back in. "Try turning it on now."

John hit the on switch, and the computer hummed to life. A message flashed onto the screen asking if he wanted his last Internet session restored. Before he had a chance to do anything, his mother grabbed the mouse and clicked *yes*. "We shall see if we've fixed the problem or if it crashes again."

The computer hummed along mechanically while the printer whirred to life. His mother clicked onto an e-mail from a contact in Kentucky. "What's this one," she said, and smiled at John. "For Christ's sake," she muttered. "What a lunatic. Listen to this. *Dear John, I am writing to you to assure you your wife is all right. I cannot give you details but please know all will be well. Although I am not certain, I am expecting you might be the recipient of a special coin. It is of no monetary value, not even American. It will appear miraculously like a lucky penny. Trust the process. This may sound crazy, but you can expect a miracle. Best wishes from a caring friend in Kentucky."*

John felt chilled. "At least this one is trying to give us hope."

"Totally insane," Jane said and added unkindly, "Your wife has certainly created a stir, but she always was a prima donna, that one. I wouldn't be surprised if she sent this ridiculous message herself. I'll erase it."

John fought his urge to throw her out of his house, mother or not. But as usual, he nodded, defeated, and said nothing, watching her smile sweetly as she deleted all the messages. He told himself there would be no real leads anyway, just like mother was telling him in that adamant voice he didn't want to hear.

John stared at the now blank screen. He needed a stiff drink. But he wasn't going to share it with his mother. "Thanks, Mom," he said. "You head on home. Dad will be happy to have you there early, I'll bet."

"He will." She beamed and patted his knee. "Things always work out for the best, son. Don't you worry. You've got a lovely baby. A son! He will be a blessing, and Daddy and I will help you raise him."

Seven: Jane

Jane held her fixed smile as she waved goodbye to her only child, John, such a silly child, and drove off down the street. The minute he was out of sight, she allowed the much more familiar frown to settle back on her prematurely lined face.

God, she needed a drink! That bitch, Seagull! How could she do this to John? Mind, she'd known all along; she'd never trusted her. The girl was too free-spirited, too outspoken and too much like...

Jane's thoughts trailed off... Too much like me at the same age is what she'd been thinking. Yes. She too had been an intelligent, free-spirited young woman when she'd met Spencer, John's father. But she hadn't abandoned her child and husband!

Why didn't Seagull realize there comes a time when you have to be responsible and settle down, especially when you have a family?

Yes, of course there is some bitterness and resentment, but it's what you do. It's what she'd done and still did!

Jane's shaky grip on the steering wheel caused her to swerve slightly, so she drove into the nearest parking lot at a Walmart's. She usually never went near such places, but necessity forced her to find a parking spot in a lane far from the entrance. The spots nearest to the doors were crammed with SUV's, a few old clunkers, but hers was probably the only Jag. Pulling up the hand-break, she turned off the engine and rested her clammy forehead on the steering wheel.

Bitch! Bitch! Bitch! She cursed Seagull while checking the time on her wristwatch. Three thirty—too early. *Not that it made much difference these days.* Jane chuckled wryly to herself. *Besides, these were desperate times.* Reaching over to her bag on the passenger seat, she felt around inside till she came across what she was looking for.

Pulling it out and unscrewing the lid, she glanced quickly around to check nobody could see her, but she was far away from the shoppers. She took a generous swig from her pint bottle of vodka. Gasping with relief as the burning liquid slid down her throat, she screwed the cap back on and waited for the shaking to subside.

Yes, the best possible outcome she could hope for was that Seagull was dead. Of course John would hurt for a while, but she would be there to help him through his agony of grief, and who knows maybe he'd have realized by then that Seagull was a passing fancy.

She'd be the one to comfort and care for him and she always would be. He didn't need a wife, not that she wanted him to be lonely—not like she'd always been. But what woman could give what a mother gave?

After all, she'd given herself up to do just that, hadn't she? Before Seagull had come along, *she* had been the only woman in John's life. All those years and time she had invested, for what, for someone else to swoop in and make her role redundant? No, no, it wasn't happening.

She took another quick swig but not wanting to get too fuzzy and knowing she ought to get back home to prepare Spencer's dinner, she tucked the bottle back into her bag, shoving it deep inside the leather sack way out of sight.

As she twisted herself around to zip it shut, she noticed a coin on the seat. *Must have fallen out of my wallet,* she thought and, with a shrug, slung it into her bag, before driving slowly and carefully out of the parking lot.

Eight: Seagull

As Seagull waited nervously outside Caitlin's office, she wondered if she was doing the right thing. She should have left Kentucky days ago, especially with her face all over the national news. She'd surely be recognized soon, despite having dyed her hair raven black, not to mention the big ugly glasses that now hid her face. She felt as if she was taking too many risks with this Jackie Kennedy fake look probably being almost as bad as returning the damn coins.

She must be out of her mind to be worried about a few worthless coins, but what if they had sentimental value? Not that she gave a damn about any of that crap—she'd left behind all of her mementos. They were a burden, nothing more. But she *had* to meet with this Caitlin woman. When she'd called her yesterday, she'd been surprised at the relief in the woman's voice. It seemed this lady was desperate to see her too. Correction, not to see her maybe, but to get back what belonged to her.

The office door opened and there Caitlin stood, tall and elegant but shifting from foot to foot, looking almost as nervous as Seagull felt. Seagull took in her attempted confident demeanor, noting the radiant but fake smile on Caitlin's gorgeous face.

Hey, who was Seagull to judge? Except, she didn't miss Caitlin's double-take at her appearance, or her slight frown, but Caitlin gestured her into the office anyway, looking politely at the floor.

After Seagull walked into the spacious office and stood in front of an executive desk, Caitlin shut the door and whispered in a hesitating voice, "Seagull?"

Seagull nodded and suddenly felt awkward and stupid. She stared out the window, unable to meet Caitlin's eyes.

Caitlin touched Seagull's arm lightly. "Sit," she said gently, indicating the chair by the desk.

Seagull sat.

Caitlin sat down too and wheeled her chair closer to Seagull, facing her, an expectant smile on her pretty face.

Seagull realized this other woman was waiting for *her* to begin the conversation, but her mind went blank. Suddenly, she remembered when she'd called yesterday, saying it was an urgent matter. What had made her say that? Somehow she managed to pull herself together, remembering the purpose for coming here. The only purpose. The coins.

She scrabbled in her bag which she'd dropped next to her feet. Damn, she hadn't even realized she'd done that. She pulled out her wallet and dipped inside. "These coins," she murmured, "I believe they belong to you." She picked out three of the coins and dug around for the fourth.

Caitlin looked concerned. "It's ok, they're not--"

Before Caitlin could finish speaking, Seagull glanced up at her, her cheeks flaming red. "I'm so sorry," she whispered. "I think I lost one."

Caitlin smiled softly, a knowing look in her eyes. "That's just it, Seagull. You didn't."

Seagull stared in confusion. What on earth was this woman saying?

Caitlin leaned forward and took Seagull's hand. "This is going to sound weird, but let me explain."

As Caitlin spoke, Seagull choked back her temptation to laugh at the ridiculous story. She had, of course, heard about the "miracle" of Caitlin's husband's son, Tommy, who'd been cured from terminal cancer. However, as a medical doctor, she was aware that cancers sometimes went into unexplainable remission and people *did* survive against all the odds. She'd also read about the premature birth by Somerville's ex-wife, who'd been held captive by a cult. It was big news at the time. A miracle people said that the baby, who everyone thought was unlikely to live, not only survived but thrived. It might be incredible but not necessarily miraculous. Medical interventions went a long way to keep preemies alive these days. What Seagull didn't understand was what any of this had to do with the four Japanese coins, three of which she was still holding. She couldn't help a slight shake of her head.

Caitlin must have noticed Seagull's doubt, because she stopped talking and was looking at Seagull with raised eyebrows.

Seagull raised her eyebrows back at the very serious face of Caitlin, and watched a faint smile appear on her lips that she quickly tried to hide. Too late, ha! Seagull couldn't help but grin.

Caitlin giggled and crossed her arms, leaning back in her chair to study Seagull. "Look," she sighed, "I know this is a lot to take in. Believe me, if anyone was skeptical, it was me."

Seagull shrugged. "I'm a doctor," she said. "There are probably logical explanations." She was about to tell her about new medical procedures, but Caitlin interrupted.

"If you'd seen what I saw, you'd know the coins in your hand have miraculous powers. I have personally seen the miracles. So, too, has my husband. In fact..."Caitlin picked up her desk phone and punched in some numbers.

Seagull sighed loudly.

Caitlin smiled, the phone to her ear. "Hey baby..."

The affection in Caitlin's voice instantly transported Seagull back to her time with John. She shifted uncomfortably in the chair, wishing she was anywhere except here witnessing Caitlin's love for her husband.

"Could you get over here? I have someone I'd like you to meet."

Seagull watched Caitlin frown at the obviously negative response to her question. She didn't want to be the cause of trouble between anyone.

Caitlin flushed slightly. "Paul, I think we can help her. I'll see you soon." Her tone was firm.

The man at the other end of the line would come, Seagull knew.

Caitlin obviously knew it too as she put the handset down and smiled. "We *can* help you," she stated simply. "You just have to believe."

Resisting the urge to snort with incredulous laughter, Seagull nodded. She *would* humor their ridiculous notions of miracle coins, letting her disdain of valueless money go. Maybe they could help her get away from here to begin a new life. If so, she'd do whatever it took. She only hoped the husband wouldn't be an ass. She vaguely remembered from the news reports he'd been a celebrity and womanizer at one time. She threw Caitlin a grateful smile and found herself really liking this sophisticated woman's kindness. She decided she might as well wait for the husband to arrive.

Nine: Seagull

Sitting in the sweeping Great-Room, Seagull couldn't help but feel overwhelmed by the opulence of this home which Caitlin had so readily opened to her. Caitlin's generosity was nothing short of awesome, as was this modern mansion with its multi-levels and white kitchen with granite counters. Every bedroom had its own bath, and there were so many windows. Seagull loved the light. Looking out, she could see willow trees near a pond and redbirds flying around a feeder. She'd seen deer too. Such gentle creatures were so peaceful, yet she felt anything but calm. The loud cawing of crows flying overhead seemed to be scolding her.

She wished Caitlin weren't so convinced the damn coins were meant for her and had some miraculous properties she somehow needed. She stacked them neatly on the end table near her chair, waiting for them to glow or do something, but apart from them being foreign, they looked ordinary. They might as well be American pennies. With those, even the copper wasn't real copper anymore, so she'd heard, and had no actual value. In fact, she understood there was talk about phasing out pennies. These coins needed to go too, except they *had* led her to a new friend and pointed her in the direction of a brand new life in, of all places, Japan.

If she could but free herself from the jitters and the guilt, she might actually get excited.

Dear Caitlin. Hard to fathom why it'd happened so fast, but Seagull already loved her. She was pretty sure Caitlin's husband, Paul, though, was as skeptical as her about the coins, but when the subject came up, he always acted noncommittal. He certainly didn't want her in his home, but he went along with his wife. He'd do anything to please Caitlin. He damn well knew he was a lucky guy. That was obvious. She *was* special. Seagull swore if she believed in such things, she'd be sure Caitlin and she were sisters in a former life! Ha. She needed to get such thoughts out of her head. She needed to be rational.

A car pulled into the driveway. Seagull's heart began to pound even though she knew it was only Paul. She didn't like being alone with him. Caitlin was at work and trusted him completely, and he'd certainly never made a pass, but she felt drawn to him. Which was ridiculous. She couldn't stand the man. She knew what he was, and she suspected he still was a philandering doper who boozed too much and hurt a lot of people.

Footsteps sounded in the entrance hallway. Seagull wanted to run somewhere and hide, but she had to face him. She recognized his firm determined stride. He was so sure of himself. So cocky. So unlike John. She ought to be grateful. Maybe today was the day he'd gotten her fake passport. She wished she liked him, but she resented all his money and how he could buy anything he wanted. She did not like rich men; maybe that's why she'd married a poor wanna-be writer who had a minimum-wage job as a dispatcher for a department store. Suddenly, in her mind's eye, John's eyes, looking doleful and sad, flashed in front of her. *Go away*, she thought. *Go away!*

"Hey," Paul said without a smile and tossed a brown envelope onto the glass-topped coffee table.

Seagull nodded to him and quickly opened the envelope. Inside was a U. S. passport. The insignia of an eagle on the front cover made her remember she'd be flying away very soon. With this document in her possession, it might even be tomorrow. Her stomach churned. She flipped open the cover, and there was a photo of her with her black cropped hair and a white streak Caitlin had insisted she add to her already weird style to give her a chic look. Seagull had loved letting Caitlin fix her hair. She and Sarah had never been that close. Sarah would probably say she looked like a punk rocker. It made her feel stupid like the rebellious teenager she'd once been, resenting her dead baby brother. She felt uneasy, too, about the name they'd given her: Jenny Johnston. It was too sweet to match the face. It wasn't her. She flipped through the pages, looking for a visa.

"I've booked you a flight—leaves Louisville in three days."

Seagull ignored him as well as her racing heart. Three days! Three days and she'd be on her way. She fumbled in the envelope, taking out an itinerary. There was another sheet of paper in there with the address of some guy called Haruo scrawled on it. He'd been involved in the weird miracle story about Paul's ex—the one who'd given birth to the miracle preemie. Probably needed to avoid him, even if Caitlin had suggested he'd put her up for a while.

Paul loomed above her, silently watching.

Seagull wished he'd sit down. "Why don't you sit?" she said.

He grunted and sank into the leather couch on the opposite side of the coffee table. He was watching Seagull's every move. She pretended not to notice but concentrated on the fact he'd bought her a round trip ticket. "I'm not coming back," she said.

"You think not. In any case, you'd need a special visa if you plan on staying longer than three months."

She stared at the itinerary. He'd booked the return flight for July Fourth. Independence Day! Was he joking? Asshole! He made her feel small and needy. "It's generous of you and Caitlin to do this for me, Paul. I don't know how to thank you, but I will pay you back once I get a job and get my life together again."

"Look." He fixed his eyes on hers.

She managed to hold his stare.

"What you are doing is foolish. And I should know. I've made some stupid decisions myself."

"You don't know me," she said, feeling herself get overheated.

"No. I realize that, but if you'll bear with me, let me tell you something about myself."

Seagull nodded, wishing he'd leave her alone. Christ, if she needed counseling, it certainly wasn't from a guy who couldn't keep it in his pants. Except he did. Now. And Caitlin, she was pretty sure, would kick him out in a heartbeat if he ever wandered. Like John did. Once. When she'd been an intern. They'd never fully discussed his infidelity. She'd blamed herself for not being available to him, too busy doing night-call and working her butt off. Her self-recriminations, she now knew, were ridiculous. John was a chump at the time and way too needy.

Paul picked up a photo of his little boy. "My first wife, Holly, is the mother of my son, Tommy." His face softened. "I almost lost this child, and I don't only mean when he almost died."

Seagull wanted him to shut up. His tender look at his little boy made her squirm. "I'm glad you like being a father, but not everyone wants to be a parent."

"What's really going on with you?" he asked, and his voice was gentler.

"I want my own life. That's all."

He shrugged nonchalantly. "I will regret forever losing Holly. I was a fool. Don't get me wrong, I adore Caitlin. She's good for me. This house was her doing. She understood we couldn't stay in the past and insisted we get our own place." His eyes got teary. "I made a lot of mistakes, and they'll haunt me forever. You want to think long and hard before you proceed, because you won't be able to undo the damage you are causing."

"I thought these worthless coins were going to make everything miraculously okay," she uttered, scowling, holding the coins up. There were now only two coins. A sinking feeling overwhelmed her. "Where's the other one?" She tried not to sound accusatory. She knew not half an hour ago there had been three coins. She dropped to her knees and crawled around searching the floor. A coin might roll on the oak hardwood, but surely she'd easily see it, yet she couldn't find it. She began checking in the pillows of the chair where she'd been sitting.

All the time, Paul observed her, saying nothing.

"Did you take it?" she finally asked. "It couldn't have disappeared. It must be here somewhere."

"It's somewhere, all right. The question is with whom. I know you don't want my advice, but if you ask me, you'd be better off staying and working out your problems. Your issues will go with you. Distance won't free you any more than booze and women ever helped me. Your life will most likely turn to shit. Running away is not the answer."

"You're right. I don't want or need your advice. I'm grateful to you for your help, but I know what's best for me." Even as she said these words, she doubted whether or not it was a good idea to go to Tokyo. But, as Caitlin had told her, she could hide there and come back once the furor about her disappearance calmed down. Maybe Caitlin had been the one suggested a return ticket on July Fourth.

Seagull's fingers detected something hard and cold under the back pillow of her chair. She knew it wasn't a coin even before she managed to get a grip on it and tug it free. A bug with a shiny brown shell wiggled between her thumb and finger. She gave a little shriek and tossed it away from her. It was a Japanese beetle.

Ten: John

It had been almost a week now, and John was going out of his mind with worry. He was sure little Lucas sensed it too. He hadn't stopped grizzling and fussing.

Yesterday, John had got close to calling his mom over again, but he just couldn't face her sharp sarcastic comments about Sea. He knew he should have called in Sea's mom, but he really couldn't face the obsessive way she doted over Lucas. Sea had told him about her lost baby brother, and that made John superstitious. He knew it was ridiculous. Lucas was a healthy child—but dear God, he was so worried about how the baby would feel to know his mother had maybe abandoned him. What would be the effect upon him psychologically from such emotional turmoil? Could he, John, be to blame? John's mom would certainly dispel any doubts about who she believed at fault, but he couldn't deal with her. He was also pretty sure he'd smelt booze on her breath the other day and couldn't stand the fact she may have gone back to drinking again. Not right now.

Oh, Sea, where are you? I need you so badly. You've always been my rock; who do I have now?

He was still receiving emails from freaks and god-fearing probably good-hearted people, but John couldn't be bothered to read them now. He knew he should simply let the police do their job. It's just he felt so useless sitting there waiting for news that might not come, and if it did, it could possibly be the worst. No, he was sure Sea just needed a break. He should have listened when she'd tried to explain how she was feeling. Instead, he'd just swept it aside, excusing her odd emotional detachment from Lucas as tiredness and the stress of a new baby.

John had let her down. He knew that now.

He heard Lucas stir in the living room and waited as his frazzled cries began. John sighed and leaned over to switch on Sea's soothing radio, allowing the music to drown out Lucas' cries. *I can't deal with him right now. He'll be fine for a few minutes.*

He leaned back against the kitchen work surface and rubbed his aching temple wearily. Despite the noise from the radio, he could still hear Lucas crying. He wasn't going to stop. *I should go to him. He needs me.* With a sigh, John headed through to the living room but stopped as he heard the chink of something falling onto the kitchen floor.

Looking down, his eyes scouring the small ceramic surface for whatever object had caused the noise, he saw a coin lying by the washer/dryer and bent down to pick it up. Behind him, Lucas screamed louder and louder. He studied the small copper piece. It looked oriental.

"Shush, Lucas, Daddy's coming!" John called over his shoulder as he continued to look at the coin. It had stirred something in him, and he narrowed his eyes, trying to think as to why it resonated so. But with Lucas screaming for his attention, he couldn't concentrate. He popped the coin into his jean pocket and went to Lucas.

John picked him up, feeling his saturated nappy in the palm of his hand and felt so guilty. *Poor boy, it wasn't his fault this was happening. He didn't choose to be born, and now it seemed not only had his mother abandoned him, but his father was neglecting him too.*

I am all he has.

"I'm sorry, baby." John held his son tight, kissing his soft downy head as his own tears splashed onto the baby. "We will find mummy," he whispered, gazing down into his little face. Lucas' crying had stilled now, and he looked up at his daddy with big trusting eyes.

John's heart skipped a beat as once again the weight of responsibility bore down on him. He needed to pull himself together. He couldn't just sit around waiting for the police. He had to do something more. That's when it hit him. He wished his computer was down here and not up in his study upstairs. The email he had received when his mom was here the other day! Somebody had said something about John receiving a Japanese coin; he remembered now.

Mom had dismissed the person who sent the e-mail as a crazy and deleted it. Oh why had she deleted it?

Why did he let her?

John set about changing Lucas' diaper and wondered if the email was still in his trash folder.

He'd sort his little boy first and check.

This could be his only hope.

Eleven: Akira

"Haruo, why can't I go to Nishimachi? I want to speak English better." Akira's voice sounded stubborn, even to him. He knew his dad would say no just as he always did. He knew they couldn't afford the school in a posh part of Tokyo, but he kept on hoping somehow tuition money might appear. He believed in miracles because he'd been one, rescued from the sea by the monk. His eyes grew sad remembering his Master who'd passed away. "Chichi," he said, aware calling Haruo "dad" always softened his adoptive father.

"You know, Akira, if I could, I'd send you there. But it is impossible for me to earn high tuition. Fishermen do not live in palaces!"

Akira hung his head. Their little apartment was plenty for him even if he didn't have his own bedroom and had to sleep on the couch. He adored Haruo but sometimes he wished he'd been allowed to become a monk. *They* had direct connection to Amida. He *knew*. Remembering the monk stirred other memories, ones he thought he'd forgotten, ones that hurt. He had no photos of his family who'd all been swept away in the tsunami, but he remembered the ocean littered with debris, and he remembered the collapsed houses everywhere, and sirens screaming.

"I'm sorry, son," Akira said. "Your school teaches English so why would this place be any better? Perhaps I can get you a tutor."

"I don't want a tutor! I want to go to Nishimachi!" Akira responded obstinately.

"I'm going to work." Haruo pulled on his coveralls and hurried out the door, sliding it shut behind him with a click.

The boy sat at the table they used for dining and also as his desk. The ancient computer monitor with its small screen took up half the space. He pressed the on-switch and went to his favorite free games site, but nothing—not the car smash game nor the roaring motorbike one—got his interest. He began to search for something new. *Hanbock Dressup* popped up—a girl's game. Akira stared at the screen. He didn't like girls, but an invasive memory of his little sister plagued him.

He hated himself for how he'd felt about Emiko. Especially now. He'd never told anyone, not even Monk, how he'd wished her dead. She'd been born when he was four, and he'd wanted a brother to play with, not a sister to be coddled. He'd wished her drowned. And when she was, he'd known it had been his fault. He'd been ten. She'd been six. He wondered if in the pure land of heaven she looked like the beautiful child she'd been named for, but the only image he could conjure was the face of a stonefish. Very ugly. Haruo cooked one last night for supper after cutting off its venomous fins. "I am so sorry, Emiko. I am so sorry, Amida," he whispered.

Refusing to give in to tears, he kicked the rung of his chair.

A coin bounced across the rattan rug.

Akira knew before he picked it up what it was—a ten yen piece. Such a common coin—could this be one of the four left in America? What was it doing here? For him? He began to smile—he would get to go to Nishimachi. Haruo would be so pleased.

Twelve: Jane

Jane stood, stirring the gravy, staring into the saucepan, yet not actually seeing it. Her thoughts were not even in the here and now, but the *then*.

The day she had received her PhD, she'd been the happiest girl in the world. Her parents and Spencer had been by her side. She'd felt like she could achieve anything. That nothing was impossible to her.

Jane had applied to a few labs, a couple of universities and even the Royal observatory in Greenwich, England. Her chosen field was astrophysics. The stars, the galaxy and the mysterious planets that were above them had always fascinated her, and now that fascination was to be her career. Her life ambition.

She'd only been seeing Spencer six months at that point and whilst she had feelings for him, Jane was far too young to consider settling down. Besides, her work could take her far and wide, and it was that freedom she looked forward to.

Spencer too had a good job, working his way up in an advertising company. He had no plans to settle either. They were having fun. Just having fun.

Until the day Jane found out she was pregnant.

Back then, it wasn't as easy as it was today. You could raise a child and have a career, but there was still a stigma, and what would her parents have thought?

Jane had been devastated and seriously considered an abortion despite it being against her beliefs. The notion that her career, her dream, was over before it had even begun, was unimaginable.

Once she told her parents, it was a done deal. They were well respected folk in the community, and for their daughter to be an unwed mother would bring upon them such shame. Jane couldn't do that to them.

The day she had told Spencer, she hadn't missed the flash of terror in his eyes, followed by the fleeting uncertainty and finally the resigned smile as he asked her to marry him.

Their wedding had been small and unremarkable. Both sets of parents had wanted something grand and fabulous, but they'd wanted to play it down, keep it simple. Like them.

When John was born, the surge of love Jane had felt for that little boy was overwhelming, and she vowed then as she still did now she would protect and care for him till the day she died.

He became her career.

When John was a little older, Jane had gotten a job, a good job in a lab as assistant. Her bosses and peers knew, as she did, that she was completely over-qualified for this work, but with a young child to care for, it was all she could commit to then.

Jane wondered if maybe when John finished college, she could apply for roles she was better suited to and would get to use her skills. But the years passed her by. Spencer's mistresses came and went, and that's when her drinking began. It took over, really. And it made her feel better.

~ * ~

"Earth to Jane!" Spencer stood behind Jane, waving his fingers in her face.

She started from her revelry. "Sorry, miles away," she muttered over her shoulder. "Dinner won't be long."

"I need the car keys."

"But dinner's almost---"

"I'm just going to the store, won't be long. Keys?" Spencer waited for Jane to complain, but she couldn't be bothered tonight. "In my bag," she said casually, still not looking around.

She heard him walk to the hall way where she always left her bag, on the dresser by the door.

As Spencer came back into the kitchen, she could hear the keys jangling. "What's this, Jane?"

Jane froze. The vodka. He'd found her vodka. *Shit! I thought I'd tucked it deep down inside my bag.* "It's not what you…" she turned to him, her cheeks flaming and stopped mid-sentence.

Spencer wasn't holding the bottle but something else in his fingers.

Jane moved closer to him to take a look.

"Looks like a foreign coin," he mused. "Oriental, I'd say." He shrugged.

"Where was it?"

"In your bag. Here." Spencer tossed the coin at Jane and she caught it, turning it over in her fingers. She had a sudden recollection of an email John had received.

As she heard Spencer slam the front door shut behind him, Jane quickly picked up the phone to call John. She ignored the hissing of the gravy as it boiled over the saucepan and onto the stove.

John didn't answer and Jane didn't bother to leave a voicemail but thrust the phone back into her pocket.

Almost immediately, her cell began to vibrate. She felt pleased that John was calling her back. So often he never responded. But it wasn't him. It was her boss calling. Jane was shaking, desperately needing to talk to John, but not knowing what she'd say to him except there was something weird going on. Could that damn e-mail be from a kidnapper? If her daughter-in-law was in trouble, a few more minutes wouldn't matter—hell, she might be dead, and you couldn't bring back the dead.

Jane had to take this call. She refused to take a chance she might lose her job. "Dan," she said into the phone. "What's up?"

"Hi Jane, I've got an interesting proposition for you."

"And what might that be?" Jane said, looking at her watch. She was in no mood for Dan's verbosity, but she had always allowed him to rattle on. "Yes, Dan," she said. "I don't mean to rush you but I'm cooking dinner and the gravy is boiling over."

"My dear," he said. "How would you like to take a temporary assignment overseas developing some specialized radio-immunoassays?"

Now, this opportunity had come. *Now!* How could she possibly leave

John in his time of need? "You know I'd love to, but this is a bad time," Jane began to mutter.

"I know, I know. It's such an opportunity for someone with your skills though. But it would probably be too far away anyhow."

Jane imagined he wanted to send her to the Arctic, which wouldn't be so bad because she'd get to see the heavens in an incredible way. "Exactly where is the job?"

"It is all expenses paid with a fat consultant bonus too. I'd go myself, but no way can I leave the lab without direction."

"Where, Dan? Where is this job?"

"It's at the Tokyo Medical University Hospital."

"What," Jane gasped, staring at the Japanese coin. "Really?" Her head was spinning. What was going on here?

Thirteen: Seagull

Seagull woke up sobbing. It had been a dream, just a stupid dream, but it had been so vivid. She could hear a baby crying but couldn't see anything. She had followed the wails in the direction they were coming from then could hear them coming from somewhere else. But everything had been pitch-black, like a midnight maze.

Seagull had sat up in bed and tried to calm herself but suddenly flinched as she felt warm liquid spilling on to her stomach. It was the milk she thought had dried up a while ago, spilling from her breasts; a natural, physical reaction to a new mother hearing an infant's cries.

She hadn't breast fed Lucas, couldn't stand him being so close. The thought had made her physically sick, so they had put him straight onto a newborn formula. Which suited her, as John could then take over all the feeding times.

This new store of milk surprised Seagull, and as she got out of bed, she groaned softly at the pain in her bosom. She would have to go and express the milk. Tiptoeing into the attached bathroom, she pulled off her nightie. Well, it was Caitlin's actually. *Oh, how embarrassing.*

She'd have to explain this little accident to her in the morning.

The morning, she thought to herself with a smile, was the day she left for Tokyo, and would be gone for good. Ha, that jerk Paul seemed to think she'd be back in a few months. No chance. The moment she got on that plane tomorrow, her life here ended and her future would begin.

Seagull gasped in relief as she eased the milk from her tender swollen breasts. It felt as if she were purging herself of any maternal substance as she watched the cloudy liquid go down the sink. Finally, when both breasts were empty, she washed herself and got back into bed. She had no idea why she was crying. She was excited. She was ready to begin again.

Still, Seagull let the tears fall, she couldn't stop them anyhow. *These will be my last, though*, she vowed as she snuggled under the quilt and found she had been inexplicably hugging her stomach.

Through the curtains, the moon shone into her bedroom and picked up the glint of the last ten yen coin that lay on the bedside table. Seagull reached across to stroke it. For as skeptical as she was, she couldn't help but feel grateful the coin *had* led her here.

Wiping her face, she closed her eyes and tried to sleep her final night in this life.

~ * ~

Seagull knew she should be grateful for Paul driving her to the airport, but she'd have much preferred Caitlin. She was such a darling. Not only had she completely understood about her nightie, she'd even bought Seagull some going-away clothes which she wore now—a comfortable green skirt which flowed down almost to the ground, a long-sleeved tee, a fuzzy green jacket and funky boots. Seagull loved her. She was going to miss her. Caitlin was such a good person—today she was directing a fundraiser for local kids.

Seagull glanced over at Paul who was whistling cheerfully, clearly happy to be getting rid of her. She couldn't really blame him. After all, he wanted his life with Caitlin and didn't need a third wheel hanging out in his house. Speaking of third wheels, Seagull thought of Jane, John's mother. She was always saccharine sweet to her face, but Seagull wasn't fooled by her faux friendliness. She'd overheard enough personal digs to John when they thought she wasn't listening. She'd tried, she really had, to win her over, but her cutting remarks always belied her brittle smiles. She was so glad she would never have to deal with Jane again.

Paul expertly pulled into the departure lane, gliding to a halt next to the Delta door. He deftly hoisted out Seagull's case—also a gift from Caitlin—and offered her his hand. "Off you go, birdie," he said with a grin that Seagull dearly wanted to wipe off his handsome face. Birdie, indeed!

"You know, don't you," he said with one eyebrow raised, holding onto her hand too long, "about the migratory habits of birds—south in the winter and north in the spring."

"I'm not coming back!" Seagull snapped.

"Just make sure you've got your ten yen piece. It's the right currency," he said, letting go of her hand.

As she marched away, dragging her wheelie, she heard him yelling to her departing back, "I upgraded your ticket to business class. Have a nice trip. See you on the fourth of July!"

Seagull could have killed him, but at least her anger distracted her from any pangs of anxiety. *Fuck you, Paul!* She took the ten yen coin out of her pocket and whilst she waited to go through security, she intentionally dropped it onto the tiled floor and pretended not to see it roll away.

Being called aboard ahead of coach class was pleasant, Seagull supposed, not that she ever wanted to be treated any different from ordinary people. But it was a relief to settle into her big seat in business. The steward stowed her case in the overhead compartment. She heard another flight attendant directing someone her way. It was a Japanese woman.

Seagull smiled.

The Japanese lady smiled back and nodded her head slightly. They chatted briefly and Seagull told her that she was traveling to Tokyo via Atlanta and LA. The Japanese woman was only going as far as LA to visit her niece who was a computer programmer.

"I'm a doctor," Seagull told her.

"Wonderful," she said. "My son and daughter are doctors too. You go visit my daughter, please. She need a friend." She took out a pen and scribbled her name and address on a note and handed it to Seagull. "You will help many people, I am sure of it."

Seagull glanced at the address in the **Nishi-Shinjuku** prefecture which the lady told her was near the imperial palace, and thanked her, grateful for another contact in Tokyo. She wasn't sure she wanted to go to the address Paul had given her, even though Caitlin had said they were good guys. Right now, Seagull wasn't much in the mood for any man.

On the second leg of the journey, their plane cruising high above the clouds on their way to LA, Seagull's newfound Japanese friend fumbled in her purse. "For you," she said. "I found it while I was waiting in the security line." She handed Seagull the ten yen coin.

Seagull's mouth fell open.

"Don't worry," the lady said in her sweet oriental accent, "it will bring you good luck."

~ * ~

When she got to Tokyo after a long flight on a redeye, Seagull was not feeling optimistic or lucky. She was exhausted and wanted to find a hotel. But she had no idea where to go. All she had was two addresses. She was also still feeling reluctant to find Paul and Caitlin's friends and happily dug out the note of the doctor's address. It was a no-brainer for Seagull to go to her. She saw her airplane friend had written something in Japanese to her daughter. She didn't understand, but it was probably something sweet, maybe an introduction. Figuring she had nothing to lose and though it was very early in the morning here, Seagull hailed a cab and showed the driver the address.

The cab flashed through the streets. Except for Japanese signs on shops, it was much like any sleeping city. They passed a Kentucky Fried Chicken and a Burger King. Seagull was looking forward to sushi and Japanese foods, not this American swill. The driver let her out next to a swank apartment complex. She asked him to wait and handed him Japanese money she'd gotten exchanged for dollars in LA.

He shrugged and pointed to the ticking meter.

Seagull smiled and grabbed her wheelie to go in search of number twenty-four which she assumed would be on the second floor. She found it and rapped on the door, but there was no answer. The doctor could be on call or anywhere, Seagull realized, and headed back to the cabbie. Sighing, she showed him Haruo's address in Yokohama.

He tsked "No go there, Missy. Not good place. Yakuza!"

"It's okay," Seagull said, thinking he was after more money, but when she offered him some, he declined.

"Get in," he said, followed by some word in Japanese which sounded musical to Seagull.

Yokohama was south of Tokyo near the sea. Its skyscrapers looked as modern as any in New York. Seagull felt quite safe and couldn't imagine why the cabbie had been so reluctant to take her to Haruo's, but when he drove down a back street not far from the docks, she began to understand. Clean and unlittered though the streets were, the apartments reminded Seagull of section-eight housing, which back home was often crime-infested.

The building where the taxi dropped her off was seedy to say the least. There were clothes hanging out on shabby concrete balconies. Seagull could smell dead fish and see a nearby dumpster which was no doubt the source of the stink. She paid the cabbie and told him not to wait. As she mounted the stairs, Seagull could hear people arguing behind the thin walls of the flat she passed. This was not how she imagined her first day in Tokyo. She had half a mind to run after the taxi and get on the first plane out of here.

Instead, Seagull sank onto the concrete steps wondering what she had done. An old Japanese man walked past her, mumbling to himself. She knew he thought her rude, getting in the way, but she was just not ready to meet anyone in this ratty apartment complex, even if they *were* friends of Caitlin's.

Seagull **leaned** against the wall where she fell asleep.

Fourteen: Akira

"It's not *that* Ten Yen piece, Akira!" Haruo sighed wearily and wiped his sweaty brow. He really didn't need this. His haul today had been poor, and there wouldn't be much money for the coming week.

"It is!" Akira stamped his feet in frustration. "I was just sitting here," he indicated the table with the computer, "and I found it."

"Loose change," grumbled Haruo, flopping onto the threadbare sofa.

Akira sat down next to him and spoke gently. "Look, Chichi, I sense something is about to happen."

Haruo cursed under his breath. "Something?"

"Yes." Akira nodded excitedly.

"You haven't heard from your monk?" Haruo rolled his eyes.

Akira smiled and patted Haruo's knee. "No, Chichi, I haven't heard from my master. He is long since passed on. However, I do pray to Amida Buddha, and I am certain I received the coin for a reason."

Haruo chuckled and patted Akira's hand. "So, your Buddha is good for something. We need all the money we can get right now!"

Akira crossed his arms petulantly and stared at Haruo.

Haruo stood up, looking away from the glare from his adopted son. "I'm going for a shower." He stopped at the computer and clicked on his inbox. "What's this?" he said, surprise in his voice. "An e-mail for me? I can't believe it."

Akira came and stood by his dad, grinning. He wanted a new computer, but he'd never complain about this old second hand machine Haruo had bought for him. It managed basic functions but wasn't very fast. He clicked on open and took a sharp intake of breath when he saw the recipient.

Paul Somerville.

Haruo saw the name too. "Now what the hell does that crazy dude want"?

Akira sat at the table with Haruo standing behind him. He read the message on his screen, translating it for his father. *"Hey crazy dudes! Here's hoping this message finds you both in good shape. Hey listen, I have a favor to ask and it's gonna sound kind of strange, but well, here goes..."*

Haruo groaned and put his head in his hands.

"It'll be okay," Akira reached his hand behind his back and grabbed Haruo's hand, gently squeezing the strong fingers.

Haruo leaned his chin on Akira's head and stared at the screen. "What does he want?"

"He says a lady is coming to visit us. An American lady called Seagull." Akira narrowed his eyes and bent forward. "Haha!" Akira's knees bounced up and down. "I knew it! Didn't I tell you? I wonder what she's like, this Seagull woman." Akira was laughing now, his smooth cheeks flushed with happiness. He jumped out of the chair and grabbed Haruo by both shoulders and shook him playfully.

Haruo shrugged him off. "Pfft! I'm going for a shower."

Much later, after Haruo had rolled out his mat in his room and was snoring, Akira couldn't stand the wait. Even the traffic noise outside, along with the various sounds of neighbors moving about, talking, coughing, yelling, had died down. He stood over his father, watching him and finally tugged on his hand. "Chichi," he asked, "why isn't she here yet?"

Haruo grunted and sat up. "Go to bed!"

"But she should be here!"

"You know it's a long way from America. Maybe she isn't coming. We have no room for her. That must be what your coin means. Now, go to bed and get some sleep. You've got school tomorrow."

Akira backed out of the small room and flopped onto the couch, pulling a blanket over his shoulders. He didn't think he'd ever get to sleep, but somehow he drifted off.

Early morning light began to light up the apartment. His eyes flew open. He heard footsteps coming down the outside corridor. He tugged on his jeans and slid open the door. A woman with black hair was coming towards him, a tentative smile on her face.

Akira flung himself towards her. "Seagull," he cried, wrapping his arms around her. "You're here!"

The lady looked surprised, but she let go of her wheelie and hugged him back. "How do you know my name?" she asked, gently moving away from him.

The boy looked puzzled. "Crazy Dude!" he cried, taking her hand and dragging her into his tiny apartment where he flipped on the old-fashioned computer monitor and clicked open the e-mail.

Fifteen: John

This was getting crazier by the minute. John gritted his teeth in anger. His mom was going to Tokyo! He needed her here to help care for Lucas—just until Seagull came home. *If* Seagull came home. He went and picked up the ten yen coin and held it up to the light. It looked like any ordinary coin, except foreign. And Japanese. This was too weird; he and his mother both getting ten yen coins out of nowhere. He wished he'd been able to recover the email about the coins. He wanted to kick himself for letting his mom take charge, deleting what wasn't hers to delete. Furthermore, she'd read the email, but of course she'd be unlikely to remember much of anything, no doubt having already hit the bottle before she got to his house. Damn booze.

He had a gut-feeling whoever sent that message might know where Sea was. She hadn't sounded sinister. Why did he know it was a *she*, he wondered? Gosh, it could as easily be a man. He groaned, tapping his forehead. *Please, please get in contact with me again*, he pleaded, *whoever you are*. He'd gone to the police station and told the duty officer about the contact, but he should never have mentioned the mysterious coins. He'd been able to tell from the cop's voice, the man thought he was losing his mind. The guy had nodded sympathetically, his eyes clouded, taken a few notes, and said he'd look into matters.

John simply could not wait for the police to make an effort to find Sea. They were probably overextended with work. One missing woman meant nothing to them. Although it cost a small fortune, he went ahead and put an open letter in *Now* magazine. He felt a little ashamed, but he'd had to accept money to pay for it from Sea's mom and dad. His chest heaved, remembering hearing his mother-in-law sobbing over the phone with his father-in-law in the background trying to console her.

He'd considered long and hard about what to write. He certainly didn't want to encourage any more weirdoes but was desperate for the sender of the deleted email to get back in touch. Maybe this plea would do the trick.

Ten Yen?

I still await news of my beautiful wife, Seagull. Our baby needs his mother and I need her too.

I think I may have inadvertently deleted an email recently and this is an appeal to the sender of that message to please get back in touch.

You see, the ten yen coins that you mentioned, I received one, as did my mother. Please get back in touch and explain the significance (if any) of this.

Do you know where my wife is? Have you seen her?

I eagerly anticipate your response. Any news, anything you know. Please get in touch.

John.

The letter, just published in today's edition, gave John some hope, but when he looked at what he'd written, he worried people would think him crazy. His wife had fucking gone missing! What possible help could worthless foreign coins be to him? It made no sense, but he couldn't help his gut feeling. He kept checking his inbox, feeling bereft at the worthless spam.

He stared at his watch. Mom would be about to board her flight. He realized she felt bad about leaving him at this time and was surprised she was actually going. Seagull would laugh and say it was about time she cut the apron strings. Seagull would laugh, too, at mom having asked his dad to keep an eye on him. His father never had much interest in him, not when he was growing up, not when he graduated from college, not ever. He certainly wasn't going to start being a decent parent now. In fact John had hardly ever seen his dad who was always working or out carousing, John realized. He remembered his mom crying and pouring herself a stiff drink. He'd wanted to protect her, but he'd only been a boy. What could he have done to make matters right between parents who were so at odds with one another? Dad was a good provider, at least, but mom ended up being both father and mother to him.

That's why being the best father to Lucas as possible was so important to him. He didn't ever want his little boy to feel unloved or neglected. Ha, laughable really, when it turned out it was Lucas's mother who'd abandoned him. Damn her! Yes, he was angry at Sea now. Of course he was also still worried, but this new emotion had kicked in. He couldn't help but think how damn selfish she was being. He struck the desktop with his clenched fist, making the computer screen wobble precariously. *Let it fall onto the floor and break into a hundred pieces*, he thought, his aggression making him feel strong and less of the pathetic wimp he suspected people thought he must be.

The ping of an incoming mail caused him to take a deep breath. His computer, currently in sleep mode, flashed into life. He quickly found the inbox. *Please let this be the one!* He opened the email, but it was another spam. All day long, time passed so slowly, he felt as if the world had stopped. He constantly checked his email. With every meaningless message, his spirits sank lower.

He managed to feed Lucas and rock him to sleep, smiling at his baby's peaceful face. *I won't let you down.* He carefully put the baby in his crib, which he'd brought into his study. He tucked a baby blanket covered with embroidered blue elephants around his son's little shoulders. Even Sea had smiled at this gift from her sister, Sarah.

Oh, Sea, where are you, he whispered, going to take a last look on the computer. Stress had drained all his energy. He felt exhausted but managed to scroll through several new e-mails. One in particular got his attention. The title was, *Friend in Kentucky*.

He sat down shakily and began to read.

John, I am the person who was in touch with you about your wife. My name is Caitlin and I work at a hospital in Louisville. Your wife was here after a car accident. Don't worry! She is fine—just a slight concussion. She came and stayed with my husband and me for a few days. I wanted her to call you and did my best to convince her she must, but she said no! I think, John, she loves you still. She said you were a good husband, but she needs her own life.

To tell you the truth, I think she's confused. She has a ten yen coin too. The fact you and your mother both have them must mean something needs to be "healed." What, I have no idea. The first miracle of the coins was when a little boy with cancer, Tommy, not only did not die as expected, but completely regained his health. I was involved in that event, and to tell you the truth, I am not and never will be the person I was before. I am so much better and happier. It's so complex. Another miracle took place for the mother of Tommy. Her unborn child was expected to die, but the baby was born perfectly healthy.

Gosh, I don't know how to explain any of this in a letter. There is a monk, or was, but he's dead now, and he seemed to be Jesus-like with miraculous powers we simply cannot understand.

Since you and your mother both got coins, then you must have some sort of mission. It will become clear to you. I am sure of that.

I know you are going to want to come rushing out to Kentucky to see me, but please don't do that. My husband is already angry about my involvement. If you show up here, it will make matters worse.

Seagull boarded a flight for Tokyo, but we have not heard from her since she got there. Here is the address of our friends who were going to put her up...

John sat there staring into space, momentarily stunned, but soon grabbed a pen and wrote down the name and address of this fellow Haruo who lives with his son Akira. His mother was on her way to Tokyo and that's where Seagull was! He immediately tried to call his mom's cell, but there was no response. She was probably somewhere over the Pacific right now where there was no cell phone service.

A sudden thought struck John. Could he trust his mother? What might she say to Seagull? She'd more than likely tell her she'd done the right thing to leave and never come back. Dear God! He'd have to arrange for Sea's mother to come here to take care of Lucas. At least he could be sure she would do a good job. He dialed up a travel site. It was way more than he could afford to buy a ticket to Tokyo, but he didn't care. He was going. He entered his credit card number and booked the next flight out of Greater Pitt.

After getting a confirmation email, he called Sea's mom, but her dad answered. "Any news?" he asked, his voice grave.

"Yes, I've got incredible news. I know where Seagull went. I'm going after her. I need Sea's mom to come here tonight and take care of Lucas."

"That's good." Seagull's father's voice sounded flat. There was a long silence on the end of the phone.

John thought maybe they'd lost cellphone service, but at last Sea's dad coughed and in a shaking voice said. "I've had to take my wife to the hospital."

John waited anxiously for his father-in-law to collect himself. He wanted to be compassionate, but right now he couldn't deal with any more drama. In just a few short months his life had gone from domestic blissfulness to chaotic hell. Everything was falling apart around him. "What happened?" he prompted, not sure he wanted to know. He had a lot of respect for this man, though. Much more so than for his own father. Sea's dad was a good guy, a family guy. His wife and daughters had been his life. Whilst Sea had always had issues with her mom, her dad had always been her hero.

"She took an overdose, John." His father-in-law's gruff voice sounded weary and hurt.

"Oh God, Pop! Is she okay?" John knew his mother-in-law, after the death of her baby boy, had suffered on and off from depression. He'd worried Seagull might be a depressive personality too, but she never had been until Lucas. Her child was alive and healthy. She had no reason. His mother-in-law sometimes needed Prozac, but she'd never, as far as John knew, gone this far.

"She's stable," his father-in-law said in a monotone. "They pumped her stomach and the psychiatrist is talking about upping her meds. Sarah's with her now. I came back to get her things. She may be in the hospital a while."

John nodded, listening intently. *Oh Sea, look what you've done.* "Can I do anything?" John asked somberly.

His father-in-law sighed. "No, John, but you should try and get Seagull back. You'll have to take Lucas with you though, I'm sorry. We won't be able to care for him right now. You understand?"

"Of course, of course." John agreed, whilst at the same time wondering how the hell he'd cope taking a young baby on a long trip by himself. "Keep in touch, okay?" He hung up the phone and looked over at Lucas, gurgling in his cot. "Hey, little buddy, how about you and me take a little trip, huh?" He shook his head in amazement at what he was about to do.

Sixteen: Caitlin

"Well?" Paul walked into the study as Caitlin shut down her lap top.

"It's done," she sighed. "I've told him all I know. The rest is up to…"

"Fate?" Paul stood in front of her walnut desk and Caitlin nodded as she looked up at him.

"You've done the right thing, Cait. You have to leave them to follow their own paths, okay?"

"I know I know," Caitlin agreed. "I just hope Seagull doesn't feel like I betrayed her."

"Babe, the guy was going out of his mind with worry and on top of that left to look after the baby, you had to put him out of his misery!"

Caitlin looked thoughtful and stood up. "I told him you'd be angry about me contacting him. I used that as an excuse to tell him not to come rushing to Kentucky. I feel like a traitor and a liar."

"You acted out of love and kindness. You didn't need to do anything. And you were right to tell John—that's his name, right—to not come here. There's nothing more for us to do."

"You're right." She walked towards her husband and fell into his embrace, loving the feel of his strong arms around her.

"Hey, it's done. Let's forget all about that Seagull woman and her family and concentrate on us from now on, okay?"

"Mmm." Caitlin snuggled her face into his neck, breathing in his gorgeous cologne.

Paul grinned to himself and slipped his hand onto her ass, pulling her closer against him.

Caitlin giggled softly and looked up at him as he bent his head to kiss her.

Moaning as desire rose up instantly inside her, Caitlin allowed Paul to push her back onto the desk as he deftly pulled her skirt up around her waist.

Delighting in this turn of events, Caitlin began unbuttoning her blouse, her gaze fixed on Paul as he stood between her legs watching her.

He lent in towards her chest and pulled aside her bra. She gasped as he gently began to tease her nipple with his tongue and she tugged urgently at his fly.

The sudden beeping of Caitlin's cell phone beside her on the desk made them both groan with irritation.

"Leave it," Paul growled as he continued to pleasure her.

But for Caitlin the moment was gone.

"I have to take it, sorry baby." She sat up and gently pushed him away as he cursed angrily and turned away with a sulk.

"Caitlin here." She waited for a response but there was only silence at the other end.

"Hello?" She waited, wondering if this was some crank call. She occasionally got them as did Paul, since the whole thing with Holly a few years ago, but they had begun to lessen lately.

Finally, a soft voice spoke. "I'm, I'm really sorry to contact you like this, but I think you may be able to help me."

Caitlin frowned, straightening her skirt as she sat down at her desk. "Who is this?"

A nervous cough was followed by a shaky reply. "I'm Sarah. I believe you have information about my sister, Seagull."

"What's wrong?" Paul asked, staring at Caitlin's shocked face.

"It's Seagull's sister," she mouthed at him then spoke into the phone, "Sarah, I didn't expect to hear from you."

"I know. John told me to leave matters in his hands, but once I knew Seagull had been helped by a woman called Caitlin from a Louisville hospital, it was easy to find you. I need to contact Sea. I'm her twin sister—and even though we aren't identical twins, I feel what she feels. I knew when Lucas was born and during the whole pregnancy she was upset, but she wouldn't say why. I can't believe she ran off like this without telling me."

Caitlin groaned. She felt an even bigger traitor. She considered hanging up, but what good would that do. "John told you Sea is in Tokyo?" she asked tentatively.

"Tokyo!" Sarah answered in surprise. "Dear God, that's where Jane is going. Jane is Sea's mother-in-law. There's no love lost between them."

"Please," Caitlin said, staring into space, wishing she'd never interfered, "how can I help? I can give you the address where she will be staying with friends of my husband's and mine."

"That would be good. And I need their phone number too."

"They don't have a phone, but here's their address." Caitlin quickly told her the address. "Are you going to go?"

"I can't. I have other family obligations. There must be some way to contact Sea faster than a letter, surely? I have some bad news, and I hate the thought of her getting it in a letter or a telegram, and I absolutely can't let Jane, her mother-in-law, be the one to tell her."

Caitlin's heart sank. "She has a new cell phone, I think. If it's got international service. You could call her."

"I've tried it, but got sent to voice mail."

"What bad news do you have to tell her?" Caitlin *so* did *not* want to be a part of this family dynamic. It reminded her of how she and her mother had been estranged and angry with one another for years.

"Our mom took an overdose. She is so fragile. I'm at the hospital now. Seagull is to blame!"

Seventeen: Seagull

In just a few days Seagull had come to love Tokyo.

The city was everything she had ever dreamed of. It buzzed with excitement, was fast-paced and exciting. She loved how she was able to get lost in the streets and crowds. Perfect.

Of course, the area where Haruo and Akira lived was a little dubious. But it was their home, and they'd been kind enough to take her in, so Seagull wasn't complaining.

Not that she could say Haruo had been particularly welcoming towards her, but Akira was a little sweetheart. *He* couldn't do enough for her. She wasn't sure what Haruo's problem was; he seemed so guarded as though he was wary of her. Still, maybe he just wasn't used to Western women. Who knew?

Anyway, Seagull had decided to cook them a meal to say thank you for letting her stay with them. Akira, the previous night, with the help of Google Translate (thank God they had Internet access) had shown her where the nearest grocery store was. She'd looked up a traditional Japanese recipe on the web, thinking it was the least she could do to cook them a dish of their native country.

Seagull strolled casually up and down the aisles of the vast supermarket. She was in no rush, the day was her own. She peered down at the shopping list in her hand. Noodles were at the top. Akira had also written the list in Japanese, so she stopped an assistant and pointed to the articulate Japanese script. The young boy pushed his glasses back up onto the bridge of his nose and looked up thoughtfully before reeling off something in Japanese.

Of course Seagull didn't understand, but she followed his hand gesture, thanking him as she went.

Reaching the aisle the young man had pointed to, Seagull stopped and stared. There were literally dozens of different types of noodles on display. She smiled to herself and began perusing the different varieties.

Then she heard the crying. It was a baby crying in the aisle next to her.

She tried to concentrate on the packets in front of her but it was no good. The baby was still crying. She felt the tenderness begin in her breasts and put down her shopping basket. Holding her hands on either side of her head, Seagull began to sing loudly to herself. She knew she must look like a mad woman, but she didn't care. She had to block out the sound of that baby crying.

She heard a young woman, its mother presumably, hushing the child in her sing song voice and it was too much. Seagull had to get out of there. Leaving the basket on the floor of the noodle aisle, she walked quickly to and out of the exit.

Once in the street, the pace seemed to have quickened and people weaved in and out of her as she wandered through the throng with the buzz of oriental accents stinging her ears. Finally, she reached a more spacious area by an ornate fountain. She stopped there and dipped her hand into the cool water, wiping her clammy forehead with wet fingers. Her heart began to slow to a steadier pace, and she was relieved to know that her breasts, so far, hadn't leaked.

She wondered at her reaction. She knew it wasn't just the physical symptoms that had shaken her so, but she didn't want to think about *that* right now. She decided to go and get a coffee before re-entering the supermarket and looked across the road for a café.

That's when she saw her hopping into a taxi.

But no, surely it couldn't have been her.

What the hell would John's mother be doing in Tokyo?

Eighteen: Akira

The headline on Yahoo didn't usually interest Akira who almost always went to his favorite game sites, but this one chilled him. There was an image of a young girl, no older than eight, who reminded him of his sister, Emiko. On closer inspection, he was sure she wasn't Emiko, but the horrible account of children, especially girls, sold for sex made him want to cry. He'd regretted wishing Emiko dead, but now he had a horrible sinking feeling she might be in a situation where it would have been better if she *had* died.

While Seagull cooked them dinner of tan tan noodles with pork and garlic, Akira couldn't get the sex slavery out of his mind, but he had to giggle at Haruo sampling the noodles with a wry grin on his face, carefully watching Seagull, who clearly didn't know these were spicy noodles. Her face turned red and her eyes watered. She grabbed the glass of beer she'd gotten for Haruo and downed it.

Haruo laughed so hard tears ran down his cheeks.

Seagull did not look amused. Her green eyes flashed, but finally she too laughed. And from that moment, Akira thought his father and this new lady would become great friends. He even hoped she might become a mother for him. While they cleaned off the plates, Akira grabbed Sea's hand. "I want to ask something."

She smiled and nodded yes. Haruo sat in their one comfortable chair watching TV.

Akira showed her the Internet article which he'd bookmarked. They soon found an English translation. "Very bad," Akira said. Then in a rush of words that Seagull clearly did not understand, he blurted out how he had a sister who'd been drowned, but now he worried she hadn't drowned but was a little girl being abused by evil men.

Seagull rubbed his back, shaking her head sympathetically.

Haruo's face became stormy. Akira knew his father, who'd been badly hurt as a child, could not abide little ones being mistreated, but he didn't expect such anger to erupt.

Haruo's fist crashed onto the table twice. "You never told me you had a sister! What is her name? We can check the death lists. If she is not dead, then we will find her. I will adopt her too. How old would she be?"

Seagull looked from one face to another obviously bewildered to see Akira burst into tears.

Haruo took the boy onto his lap. "Hush," he said. "If she is alive, we will find her."

Seagull went to them and wrapped her arms around the boy until his sobbing eased. She slowly backed away, her own eyes full of tears. "What can I do to help?" she asked in her broken Japanese.

"My sister," Akira cried. "I wished her dead and now she comes to haunt me. On my way to school I saw little girls with yakuza thugs but didn't understand," he wailed. "What if one of the little girls is Emiko?"

Nineteen: Jane

What a wonderful feeling it was to wake up without a hangover. It was Jane's second day in Tokyo, and she hadn't touched a drop of drink. She hadn't needed to. Her initial nerves about this trip had proved unfounded. The idea of traveling used to be so important to her when she was a new graduate, but now it scared the shit out of her. But Jane knew she could do this. Even if it wasn't astrophysics, she was a damned good biochemist and had nothing to prove.

Yesterday, Jane had met with the man that headed up the team she would be working with at Tokyo Medical University. Fumio seemed like a nice guy. He was clearly intelligent, judging by the way he talked about the work of his team and what he expected from her. She thought he was younger than her, though it was difficult to tell from his clear smooth face. Jane had earned the wrinkles in her face but thought she might just get a Botox treatment to feel young again. Fresh. Why shouldn't she look good?

This project was something Jane felt she could really get her teeth into. She was unconcerned about it being so unlike her hopes for meaningful work when she'd first gotten her PhD in astrophysics. Stars and constellations be damned. This work was perfect. The assay they would be working on would finally enable her to apply her math skills and if successful, could see them discovering a new and more effective way to pinpoint cancer cells and apply focused chemotherapy. Jane would start the job properly on Monday morning. Yesterday was an informal chat and today was Saturday, so she had the weekend to familiarize herself with the city before she immersed herself in the research.

She switched on the computer in her hotel room, thinking that she really should check on John. Sure enough, there was an email from him.

As she began to read, Jane's heart started beating so fast she could feel an artery in her neck fluttering.

Hey Mom,

If you're reading this, I'm guessing you got to Japan okay. I hope you had a good journey.

Mom, listen I found out where Seagull is! She's there in Tokyo, with you.

I've booked myself and Lucas onto a flight, so by the time you read this, I'll probably be half way to you.

Believe me, I am going to fetch Seagull home, but not before giving her a piece of my mind, and insisting she get into therapy.

Mom, I spent a lot of money on these flights, so I was hoping you'd be able to let us stay with you at your hotel/apartment.

Thanks Mom, see you soon!

J.

Jane's pulse was so high she felt dizzy, and she bet her blood pressure was through the roof. Goddamn them both, including John. How could they be such idiots? John certainly knew better than to go dragging Lucas across the Pacific. As for Seagull, when would her son realize she was an irresponsible prima donna who he was better off without?

This was supposed to be *her* time. *Her* opportunity. She had dedicated her whole life to raising John, and now she had this moment for herself, but he was intruding on that too. Well no! She wasn't having it. He knew where Seagull was so he could damn well find her. Without his mother! She wouldn't reply to his email; she wouldn't take his calls either. This was a busy city. Jane was going to make sure he didn't find her.

A chuckle rose out of Jane's throat involuntarily. What an irony. John might find his wife and maybe she'd repent, but even if she did, he was about to lose his mother. Fair trade-off, if you asked her. He could have that witch, but he couldn't also have her. It didn't work that way. At least not until she'd had time for herself, her *me* time, her *be me* time without anyone to burden her with their needs.

Not for long, just for long enough for Jane to have her moment. Switching off the computer, Jane glanced at her watch. Ten thirty. Too early? Who cared? Who would even know? She left the room and headed for the hotel bar.

Twenty: John

John was fucking exhausted. Lucas had cried and fussed on the flight out of LA to Tokyo. John supposed he should feel grateful he'd been quiet from Pittsburgh to the west coast, but one thing caring for a baby had taught him was to be present for every moment. He had longed for his crib and more help. Sure, the flight attendants had been kind, and a woman across the aisle from them had done her best to soothe Lucas, but John still heard the exasperated sighs of people in the seats behind them. He didn't blame them, but it was too bad.

Lucas was cranky. Now so was John. The airport, even at this early hour, was full of people. He didn't even have any Japanese currency, but he saw a monetary exchange booth. There was a long line, but he had to get some yen so he could go to Jane's hotel. He couldn't believe she hadn't responded to his texts.

At last it was his turn and John handed the clerk $200. It was all he had, and he had a feeling it wouldn't last long in this city. He'd heard it was one of the most expensive in the world. John sighed as the clerk gave him some notes and coins. "Can you tell me the best way to get to Mandarin Oriental Hotel?" he asked and tried to show him the address he had written down on a post-it note. It wasn't easy to fish it out of his pocket whilst holding the baby, who was, thank God, asleep.

"Please step aside, sir," the clerk told him, not bothering to answer his question.

Fortunately for John, there was a young man who bowed and told him which subway to catch. The man wrote down the directions in English: subway *"Mitsukoshi mae station" A7 exit directly.*

John had to take a shuttle bus from Narita Airport to Tokyo station. He wasn't sure, with Lucas in one hand and a bag of diapers in his other, how he would have managed if another Japanese guy hadn't helped him get his duffle bag onto the bus. It had been bad enough trying to maneuver through the crowds.

At last he was crammed onto a subway train which was flying through the tunnels. John finally saw the A7 exit flash up and he dragged himself, Lucas, and all their gear onto the platform. Just at that moment, Lucas woke up and began to fuss. John had a carton of baby formula to give him and felt eternally grateful to the customs woman who had let him bring it through. He sat on a bench while Lucas sucked away greedily. Then he burped him before they set out.

The hotel lobby where his mom was staying was modern and clean looking—simple but very elegant. John knew his mother must love this place. He couldn't wait to get up to her suite and rest. He walked wearily to the desk where two uniformed clerks were on duty. "Could you let my mother, Jane Hudson, know I'm here. She's in suite--"

"Sorry, sir," the clerk answered with downcast eyes. "She checked out an hour ago."

"What? That can't be right. Where would she go? Did she leave a forwarding address? She must have."

The clerk shuffled through some papers on his desk. "No, I'm sorry, sir. No forwarding address. She paid her bill and left. That's all I have."

Lucas suddenly began to bawl, and John could smell his diaper beginning to stink. He had no idea what to do next. He felt angry, tired, and downright fed up. He spotted a little girl with big eyes watching them from the central lounge. She looked sad and something about her tugged at John's heart, but he had no time for anything except to change Lucas who was crying even harder and had spat up on his shoulder. To hell with what anyone thought. They could throw them out, but first he was going to take care of his baby. John lay Lucas on a couch and began changing him.

The little girl was still nearby and smiling shyly. John couldn't help but smile back. Her father, who was elegantly dressed, looked at John critically, but then he bowed slightly and moved closer—too close for John's comfort. The man waited until John had finished taking care of Lucas. His presence was making him uncomfortable. At last, he spoke in flawless English. "She will make you a good child minder." He took the little girl by the shoulders and spun her around as if she were for sale.

It hit John suddenly that she *was* for sale. He wanted to call the police, but he had too much going on to take on anyone else's problems. He was tempted to go to the desk and demand they do something, but they were none too friendly. "I'm sorry," he said to the little girl who was so pretty in spite of the red birthmark across her nose. John figured she wasn't much older than eight. Surely he must have been mistaken and her father was making polite conversation. He was getting really paranoid. Too tired. Too much stress. He fished out the address for Haruo and Akira. "How do I get here?"

The man walked away, dragging the little girl along next to him.

Somehow, John gathered everything and went back to the subway where he proceeded in what he hoped was the direction towards Yokohama.

John's heart began to beat fast when he walked up the stairs of a cheap housing complex and down a narrow concrete walkway towards the apartment where he expected to find Sea. He had no idea what he would do or how she would react. Lucas was beginning to cry again, no doubt sensing John's anxiety. He tapped on the sliding door and it quickly slid open. A young boy with big eyes stared at John.

"I'm Sea's husband," John said. "And this is our baby, Lucas."

An older man looked over the boy's shoulder. "She's not here," he stated, but the boy grabbed John's hand and tugged him into the apartment. It was tiny and there was no sign of Seagull. "This is our baby," John repeated. "His name is Lucas. You must be Akira and Haruo."

The man grunted and glared at him. "She leave her baby?" He looked as if he'd swallowed a shark.

Twenty-one: Seagull

Seagull was in the tiny bathroom of Haruo's apartment where she could hear John in the living area. Thank God Caitlin had warned her John was on his way. And with Lucas too! Jesus, what had he been thinking taking a tiny baby on such a long haul?

She could hear Lucas crying. Could he sense her near? Oh God, what had she done? She'd just wanted to get away, to start afresh. Now all her physical urges were kicking in, her breasts were tender, and Seagull just knew they were going to leak. Her heart was pounding in her chest, and she wasn't sure if it was from fear of John finding her or that she wouldn't be able to resist going to her son.

There, she had said it: her son. Her baby boy.

His cries were getting more urgent and were all she heard over John's murmuring conversation with Haruo. She should go to him, she thought, as she felt a trickle of milk drip down onto her torso. Seagull knew she *should* go to him. But then this would all have been for nothing.

What to do?

She put her hands over her ears, unable to bear the torture.

Haruo's sudden raised voice made Seagull jump. *"She left her baby?"* She heard him say. Oh God. He was never going to help her now.

"She not here. Go!" She heard little Akira trying to salvage the situation but feared it was too late. Lucas was screaming and making the already panicked situation even more frantic.

Shush baby boy, she silently willed her son, hoping that despite their lack of a bond, he'd somehow hear his mother's wishes. Miraculously, Lucas stopped crying, though Seagull was sure it was less to do with her and more that nobody was paying him much attention anyway.

She continued to listen.

"Yes, she left her baby! Why do you think I'm here? Did she not even mention us to you?"

Seagull sighed. Thank God Haruo didn't speak much English.

"Go! She not here!" Little Akira spoke again.

"Look." She heard John sigh wearily and had a sudden instinct to hug him.

"Here's my cell number. Call me if you hear anything, okay?"

Haruo grunted and Seagull heard Akira ushering John and Lucas out of the door.

Her husband and her son. Her family. She wanted to run to them. She needed to scream how sorry she was. That she was a useless wife and an even worse mother. Instead, Seagull stayed where she was, crouching beside a dirty toilet in a run-down apartment in one of Tokyo's worst districts. Because here, at least, she felt safe.

Akira tapped on the door. "You okay?"

Opening the door, Seagull peeked out. "No, not really."

She walked into the living area, and Haruo frowned at her. "Why did you leave your baby? You only said you left your husband. I thought he was a creep."

Akira translated and Seagull hung her head in shame. "I don't know. I have to be me." It sounded like a lame excuse, and the look on Haruo's face when Akira relayed her words told Seagull he was angry. He began to yell Japanese words which she knew were expletives, intentionally ugly. They were directed at her, and she crumpled onto the couch. Akira sat next to her, stroking her back as Haruo tugged on his fisherman coveralls and stormed out of the apartment without a goodbye.

Seagull knew she couldn't stay here. John was bound to come back.

Suddenly, she remembered the doctor lady who hadn't been home. Praying she'd kept her address, Seagull fumbled through her suitcase and was relieved to find she still had it. Thank Christ. She would go to her. No one else knew anything about her and she wouldn't even tell Caitlin where she'd gone. Why should she? She'd had no business interfering, giving Seagull's address to John. Sarah probably had it too. God forbid if she were to show up here.

There was a ding on Seagull's phone. Talk about déjà vu! It was Sarah. Caitlin must have given her the cellphone number. The text said, *"Mom hospital again. Overdose. How could you leave without a word?*

Twenty-two: Jane

It was Monday morning and the alarm had just gone off. Jane opened one sleep-encrusted eye and hit snooze on her phone.

Oh Shit! She had to start the job today and she felt crappy.

Jane had spent much of the weekend getting wasted. She had checked out of her hotel yesterday morning and had somehow ended up renting this little apartment. It wasn't in a very nice district, and she didn't know why she had chosen it. Mind, she'd been pretty drunk when she'd entered the office of the estate agent. She was so grateful for the Google translation app. Jesus, how else would she have managed? Although many Japanese speak good English, this area was quite poor and aside from this particular drunken lush turning up at their door, Jane didn't imagine the agency leased to many westerners.

Still, it was home for now. She peered out of the little grimy window and sighed. A smoggy day was beginning, and the local stall holders were setting up for market day. That explained the aroma of smelly vegetables and rotten fish that invaded Jane's nostrils.

A young woman shuffled along the street, pushing her baby in its buggy. Jane suddenly thought of Seagull. What was wrong with her? How could you not bond with your baby? John was her everything from the moment he had been born. He and Lucas would have arrived by now. She wondered what his reaction had been when he'd been told she'd left the hotel.

No doubt there was a text message from him on her phone, but Jane couldn't be bothered to check yet. She needed to shower and freshen up to get ready for the day, and she didn't feel a bit guilty about avoiding him. He needed to stand on his own two feet. Racing across the world to find that silly wife of his! Mind you, she did worry for little Lucas. Maybe she should let John know where she was.

Deciding to check her phone after all, Jane was shocked to see six missed calls, all from John! Good Lord, had something awful happened? Her maternal instinct was back, and it kicked her in the stomach with a massive dose of guilt.

She quickly called John's number, knowing she'd never forgive herself if something had happened to either of them.

"Mom! Where the hell are you?"

Jane sighed. "Doesn't matter. I'm fine. Are you both okay?"

"We're fine. I got us the cheapest hotel I could find, but mom I'm running out of money and I can't find Sea!"

Rolling her eyes heavenwards, Jane listened to John's anxious speech then heard Lucas crying in the background. "Is Lucas okay?" She interrupted her son.

"What? Oh he's just hungry, Mom. Where are you?"

She knew she should tell him; it was unfair not to. He needed her right now. "I don't know where I am, John, but I'm going to find myself. I'll call you soon." Jane hit the "end call" button on her cell and switched off the phone. Then she got ready for work.

~ * ~

When she arrived at the medical center, Jane felt a little apprehensive. Could she do this? Her confidence had suddenly deserted her, and she considered turning around, collecting her belongings and getting on the first flight out of here.

"Jane, good to see you. You ready to start?"

She turned at the greeting and smiled nervously at her Japanese boss and colleague, Fumio, who offered her his hand. Shaking it, Jane relaxed slightly at the warmth in his eyes and followed him across the reception to the elevators where they stood and waited.

"How are you finding Tokyo?" Fumio asked politely.

Jane nodded enthusiastically. "It's great!" Privately, she thought of how the booze was bloody expensive though.

They continued to make small talk as they rode the elevator up to the fourth floor, and Jane began to feel much better as Fumio took her into his office. She couldn't help but notice the photo of a pretty woman on his desk and found herself wishing it was her. But that was ridiculous, she was at least ten years older than Fumio and besides she was a married woman and had sworn never to become like Spencer, a philanderer and betrayer.

After some discussion about the research, Fumio gave Jane an extensive tour of the lab. It was equipped with the finest and most modern equipment, and there were three research assistants, all of whom spoke English and were busy using micropipettes, so very familiar to Jane. Her job would be to work with one of the young men and show him how to carbon-date the enzymes extracted from monkey blood.

Instead of using live animals for research here, they used, of all things, scrapings from human toenails as their basis. Jane's heart soared—she had always hated seeing the monkeys in their cages, obediently sticking out their arms to give their blood. Well-treated though they were, she had so wanted to return them to their native lands.

Jane was beaming by the time she left the lab with an armload of scientific journals, including Fumio's PhD thesis, to get her up to speed with the other members of the team.

Team! She loved it.

Fumio grinned at her, his teeth white and even in his kind intelligent face. Gripping her hand for a little too long, Jane felt herself stirring in ways she knew she ought *not* to be stirring. Surely she was imagining this. She refused to let anything get in the way of the work. The work was all that mattered. They might come up with ways to save hundreds, maybe thousands of lives.

"It would give me great pleasure if you would join me for dinner this evening," Fumio suddenly said with a sweet smile.

Jane nodded. "I'd love to come," she accepted enthusiastically, excited at the prospect of an authentic Japanese meal and it would be good to meet his wife. He could even have kids, but she hadn't seen any photos of children in his office amidst his various diplomas and awards.

Giving Jane directions to his apartment which was in Nishi-Shinjuku District, not too far from the medical center, Fumio told her what time to come and assured her she needn't bring anything but herself.

Back at her flat, Jane checked her phone for the first time since this morning. Damn. There was another string of texts from John. She had a good mind to ignore him completely, but maybe she could simply give him her credit card and bail him out financially. She really was tired of having to take care of him as if he were a baby. For crying out loud, he was close to thirty.

Later when Jane arrived at Fumio's address, she felt suddenly nervous. The area was so much nicer than the dank market one she was living in. But it wasn't just that. She worried about the *moment* she had felt with Fumio today and concerned that after a few drinks she wouldn't be able to hide her attraction to him in front of his wife.

Walking up the short flight of steps to his door, Jane decided to remain sober tonight. Just in case.

Taking a deep breath, she rapped lightly on the shiny white door of Fumio's home.

Fumio opened the door with a grin, and she smiled back with a brightness that belied her nerves.

"Come in, come in." Fumio stood back to allow her to enter, and Jane quickly bent to remove her shoes. She saw the appreciation in Fumio's face as she stood and she offered her gift to him, with both hands. Yes, she'd done some research before tonight!

"For your wife," Jane said as she proffered the present. It was a little pair of owls, an animal considered lucky in Japan.

Fumio crinkled his brow as he accepted the gift with a nod. "My wife?"

Jane's heart sank. *Oh God, had she insulted him in some way?* She thought she had thoroughly researched the social etiquette in this country.

Fumio noticed Jane's horrified face and smiled warmly. "I am not married, Jane."

She sighed inwardly with relief that he was not offended but felt suddenly confused.

"But I thought…" She trailed off as Fumio placed his arm around her shoulder and guided her into the living area of his spacious apartment.

"Ah, the picture on my desk?" It was a rhetorical question, but Jane nodded all the same. "That is of my sister, Asa. Drink?" Fumio pulled a bottle of champagne from the ice bucket on the table in the living room and Jane nodded, instantly forgetting her earlier vow.

"She is very beautiful," Jane smiled as she accepted the cold glass of fizz from him.

As he passed the glass, Fumio's hand trembled momentarily, and Jane looked at him with concern.

"She is," he said quietly, looking to the floor. "She is beautiful," he continued, "but she's very unhappy. Her family died in the great Tsunami."

Jane gasped as her hand flew to her mouth.

"I'm so sorry," she said, and Fumio brushed the air with his hand as if to tell her it was okay.

"Her husband and three children, all gone." Fumio looked at Jane with sad eyes, and she didn't miss the watery sheen of unspent tears in them.

"That's horrible," Jane remembered the footage on the news of that horrendous wave which had wiped out so many.

Fumio nodded then stood up straight. "Dinner!" he announced, telling Jane that, for now, that was the end of the conversation.

As he walked to the spacious kitchen area of his open planned home, Jane took in her surroundings.

She was impressed with the art work on the wall, recognizing some of it as expensive pieces. *I like it here. I feel comfortable,* she thought, as she sipped her drink.

"Sit, please," Fumio called over his shoulder, and with a contented sigh, Jane sank into the soft white leather sofa.

Watching him as he expertly chopped vegetables and threw them into the wok, adding various spices and oils as though it were second nature, she couldn't help comparing him with Spencer, who could barely grill a steak. Jane realized Fumio had noticed her staring at him and quickly averted her eyes. "Great art work." She nodded at the walls and Fumio grinned.

Shit, this was awkward!

She slugged back the rest of her drink, hoping he'd top her glass up soon.

Twenty-three: Seagull

"Please don't go," Akira begged, his dark eyes full of tears.

"I have to. Your father doesn't want me here."

"He'll come round. You'll see."

Seagull turned away from the boy, unable to bear his despair any longer. "It's not just that," she murmured. "I must not be found."

"Why?"

When Akira stamped his foot petulantly, she faced him again. "Just because. Okay?" How could she explain anything to this child when she didn't understand her own confusion? She hurried to the small alcove that had been her makeshift bedroom and began throwing her things into her hold-all.

Akira sobbed quietly.

Seagull wished she could block out the little boy's hurt feelings. It was all she could do not to burst into tears too. Akira was such an adorable child. She couldn't understand how she could feel love and compassion for someone else's kid but not for her own.

"I'll see you again. Soon," she said, walking out the door, choking back tears. Akira didn't even look up from his crouching position with his head in his hands. She ached to turn around and go to him, and hold him tight, but she couldn't. She just couldn't!

After stepping outside, she stood perplexed, next to the dank building. She didn't have much money and didn't want to spend it on a cab but had no idea which buses she needed to take. At last, she went to a bus stop and when the first bus pulled up, showed the driver the address on the note. He beckoned her on board and told her where to get off, pointing at another bus and saying something in Japanese. The bus he'd pointed out displayed

Japanese numerals she couldn't understand.

When a couple of people came rushing up to catch the bus, Seagull hurried after them and once again had to show the driver her address. He grinned and beckoned her on to the vehicle, refusing to take her money for the fare. He let her off outside the place where she'd been before. She breathed a sigh of relief. But *now* that she wasn't struggling to find the right bus, remembering Akira's tears, she began to shake. She doubted she'd be able to trace her way by bus back to his apartment even if she wanted to. And she did want to. She did! But how could she with John prowling around?

She waited a few moments to collect her emotions then dragged herself up to the second floor and rang the doorbell. It sounded like wind chimes. *Please be home*, she thought, waiting for what seemed like five minutes but was probably no more than a minute.

At last, the door slid open and a petite Japanese woman stared at Seagull. "Yes," she said brusquely in English.

Seagull explained how she'd met her mother on the plane to LA. "Your mother gave me your address and asked me to stop to see you."

"I can't imagine why," the woman said rudely but gestured for Seagull to come inside.

"I need a place to stay," Seagull blurted.

"Very well." The woman nodded curtly. "I will show you around."

Unlike most Japanese Seagull had met, this woman did not smile at all, yet her English was flawless. Seagull wondered if her mother had gotten in touch with her or if they were estranged. She didn't want to be in the middle of more domestic strife. She also wondered why this woman was showing her around unless she hoped to convince Seagull there was no room for her to stay.

Seagull humbly walked after the woman throughout the small but modern apartment. The woman's Japanese voice sounded cold and unfriendly, making Seagull wish she hadn't come, except she had nowhere else to turn. The cool décor with its dark wooden floors and stark white furnishings seemed to reflect the owner's temperament. The apartment certainly didn't bespeak a warm person, but Seagull realized she had no right to judge her without even knowing her.

"You may stay the night," the lady said at last, showing Seagull into a tiny room not much bigger than a closet with a pull-out bed.

"Thank you so much." Seagull almost promised to not be a nuisance, but her hostess pointed to the cot and hurried away into the main room.

Seagull sat silently, expecting her to come back and offer her tea or something, anything, but she didn't come. Every so often, Seagull could hear her shuffling papers. *Why didn't she ask about her mother? Surely, even if they weren't on speaking terms, she'd want to know how her mother was doing?*

Perhaps they had something in common. Perhaps this woman had deserted her family too. Seagull felt herself begin to perspire, remembering the woman's mother had written something to her daughter in Japanese. She could only hope that would please her. Seagull found the note with the name Asa scrawled in English above some Japanese words.

Clutching the note, she stepped into the small living room. She should have given this to her hostess right away, but for all she knew, Asa was not her name.

"Asa?" she asked tentatively, staring at the emotionally distant lady who sat at a desk in the corner of her living room. Her long silky dark hair had fallen over one shoulder as she squinted in concentration at a paper she'd been reading. The desk was piled high with tattered medical journals and bundles of paper tied with pink string.

"Yes," the woman said, turning to face Seagull.

Seagull felt like a high school girl having to see the principal for misbehavior. "Your mom wrote something to you in Japanese." She held out the scrap of paper. "I should have given it to you right away. I'm sorry. I was distracted."

Asa glared at her and reached for the note, reading it with a little frown on her face. She crumpled it into a ball and dropped it into a tiny wicker wastepaper basket.

"She really had no business giving you my details."

Seagull wanted to ask what her mother had said or did to make her respond this way, but of course she said nothing. Despite Asa's coolness toward her, Seagull liked her. Well, no, maybe she admired her. She was beautiful, intelligent; she was her own woman. She was everything Seagull wanted to be. "So," she cleared her throat nervously, "You're a doctor too?"

She added the *too* more to establish herself as a professional than anything. For some reason, Seagull wanted her to know that she wasn't some dumb American broad with issues. She wanted her to know that they were not so different.

"Mmm hmm, I am a doctor," she replied, looking back at her paper.

Seagull clenched her teeth. How dare she dismiss her as if she didn't exist? She tried again. "What do you practice?"

Asa sighed and spun around in her chair, finally locking her dark eyes on Seagull. "I'm a pediatrician."

Seagull felt a blush rise on her chest that threatened to creep up her face. This woman looked after children. *Oh God, she can't know what I've done, can she?* Seagull mentally flipped back through her conversation with her mother on the flight over and was certain she'd never hinted at being a mother herself, least of all a neglectful one.

Asa was still staring at Seagull, but her gaze softened. "How old was your baby?" she whispered, blinking in the fading light of the room.

Seagull gasped. "How did you…"

Asa smiled knowingly and stared at her still swollen breasts.

Seagull let out a small breath and nodded slowly, acknowledging that, of course, she would have noticed.

Her eyes were burning into Seagull's, making her feel even more flustered. "He is called Lucas," Seagull said quietly as her eyes watered and her breasts began to ache.

For what seemed like a very long time Asa said nothing, just studied her, making her feel uncomfortable. *What is she thinking? What judgment is she making of me?* Seagull wanted, no needed to explain. Asa was a woman, surely she would understand. "He's, I…" she stumbled with her words.

Before she could continue, Asa raised a slender hand in the air to stop her. "You said *is*."

Seagull, her brow furrowed, her head tilted, didn't know what she was getting at. "Excuse me? What?"

"You said *is* not *was*. I assumed your baby was dead." Asa said this so matter-of-factly Seagull groaned out loud.

"No, no…" Seagull walked towards the other woman, but she put up both hands to stop her mid-stride.

"So you left him." This was a statement rather than a question.

It knocked the wind out of Seagull. She stepped back.

Asa gave her one final look up and down before turning back to her work.

Seagull knew the conversation was over.

Twenty-four: John

"Lucas, honey." John cuddled his darling baby in his arms and rocked him, jiggling him up and down. "Shssh. We'll find your mommy. I promise." His calm soothing tone belied his real feelings.

Lucas had been crying non-stop all night, and nothing seemed to calm him down. John didn't have a thermometer but worried the baby might have a fever. If only he spoke the fucking language, maybe that would help. How, he didn't know, but at least he wouldn't feel so helpless and alone. Mom refused to take his calls. All he knew about her whereabouts was she'd be working at a medical center. Sea was nowhere to be found. He'd almost run out of money and feared his credit cards would soon be rejected. The only thing keeping him going was the need to be strong for Lucas, but if he could, he'd catch the next plane home. With or without Sea. Fuck his mother too.

The cheap hotel stank of mildew. Damn well couldn't be healthy for a baby. Soon John gathered the baby and all the luggage and stood on a sidewalk wondering where the hell to go. He could try to find Jane at the medical center, assuming there weren't scores of hospitals, but what help could she be? She'd always interfered in his life and his marriage, but now when he actually *wanted* her help, she'd made herself invisible. What kind of mother was she, leaving him and her grandson in the lurch when she could so easily have put them up at her hotel? Instead, he thought grimly, she did a bunk when she knew they were coming. She was as bad as Sea. *Damn you, Sea. Where the hell are you?*

He had nowhere to go but back to that seedy apartment. It was within walking distance from here. He'd like to give that surly Haruo guy who'd been so rude to him, shouting at him that Sea wasn't there, a piece of his mind. What had he done to deserve the guy's anger? The man could at least have been hospitable. John would have invited any stranger who'd traveled so far into his house for a cup of coffee or a beer. Now he wished he'd gone into the joint and searched the place. Maybe they were protecting her. As if he posed a threat. Ridiculous!

As he walked along, dragging his case with one hand, cradling Lucas in his other, the baby blessedly having cried himself to sleep, he couldn't help but notice the poverty. This was a rotten neighborhood oddly free of litter but full of decaying buildings. People stared suspiciously at him. No doubt his Levi jeans and fairly new athletic shoes looked expensive to them. To tell the truth, he was afraid someone would try to rob him. And since he had nothing of value to give them, they'd probably kill him. He held onto Lucas tighter and picked up his pace until he arrived back at the high-rise. He leaned against a low wall for a while and rested. He felt like a cop surveying a crime scene. This place, this area, gave him the creeps.

Damn, here came that kid, Akira, shuffling along like an old man, staring at the ground. He waited until the boy was almost up to him before stepping forward. "Hey, kid, remember me! Tell me the truth. Has Sea been staying with you?"

The boy looked startled and raised his eyes briefly. He looked as if he was about to run away, but John let go of his suitcase and grabbed his arm to make him stay. He sank against the wall next to John.

"She's gone," he said. "I don't know where." He looked tearfully at Lucas. "This her baby?" His English was broken but understandable.

"Yes. His name's Lucas," John replied.

The boy stroked the baby's head. "He pretty baby."

John's heart warmed to this kid. He looked closely into his sad eyes and smiled. "You on your way to school?" He'd noticed the kid's backpack full of books.

Something in the boy's melancholy face reminded John of the little girl in the hotel who'd looked at him so hopefully when her father tried to get him to hire her as a child-minder. This kid had a red mark across his nose too—not as noticeable as the little girl's, but he swore they could be brother and sister. The longer he looked at the kid, the more he thought the resemblance might be real. More than likely, though, he was jet-lagged, overwrought, and now inventing foolish similarities. His stomach began to churn at the thought that no decent father would try to pawn his daughter off onto a stranger.

He had no idea why he asked this, but the question popped out, "Kid, do you have a little sister?"

Twenty-five: Seagull

"Jesus Christ!" Seagull cried, awaking from a nightmare, saturated with sweat. Her breasts were leaking. She couldn't stop trembling. For a moment she didn't even know where she was. But then she remembered. Asa's flat. She had a roof over her head, but oh such a chilly place. Who was this cold woman, she wondered? What the hell went on in her life, but Sea's nightmare soon made her stop wondering about the reasons for *her* angst. She had enough problems of her own.

In her dream she'd been alone, with monstrous images looming around her. In one episode, she was a decapitated but alive person crouching in the corner of a strange room. She wanted to flee but couldn't. In another version, she lay in a deep hole, and people were after her, looming outside, guns at the ready.

Her heart rate began to slow, and she could think a little better. *Did she cry out? Did Asa hear her?* If she did, she was not bothering to come to see if Seagull was okay. Seagull couldn't really blame her.

What if the dream had been an omen about Lucas? Maybe the baby was in trouble? Should she go to him? Christ, she wished she knew what do to, but the truth was there had been an image in the dream of a child, not of her baby but of Akira. *Why was she so upset about a boy with a father who loved him? Why was he appearing in her dreams?* She almost couldn't stand the memory. She knew people repressed dreams and she wanted to repress this one of that dear little dark-haired boy who was loving and kind and was her friend. *He doesn't need me, does he?*

What the fuck is going on?

Her confused memory of her dream got clearer. She saw Akira, his hands over his face, screaming a name she didn't understand. She didn't recognize the name he was crying, but as she lay there on this tiny cot, it became clear. *Emiko, Emiko, Emiko* she heard echoing in her brain. She wanted to blank it out. She couldn't stand the agony. "Asa," she groaned. "Asa!"

The petite Japanese woman slipped silently into the tiny closet of a room and put her cool hand on Seagull's forehead. Her face seemed to glow in the light with an aura of *what,* Seagull couldn't tell. But she trusted her. "I need your help," she managed to say. "It's not just me," she begged.

Asa stroked Seagull's brow. "I know," she whispered, tears rolling down her cheeks.

Seagull looked up into her face and realized the coldness in Asa's eyes was far more than the look of someone aloof who wanted to be left alone. Her eyes seemed full of loss, tragedy, grief. "Tell me," Seagull whispered into the darkness. "What has you so upset?" She held her breath, waiting to be told to mind her own business.

Asa looked at her thoughtfully as if she were debating whether or not she wanted to share her misery with a stranger, one who might well not be ready to hear it. But she cocked her head slightly and cleared her throat. Sitting quietly on the side of the cot, her hip against Seagull's feet, she told her story.

"I too had a son. A whole family in fact. My husband and I took our three children, my son and two daughters on vacation. Goro, my husband, was working a lot of late nights, so we decided to have a few days away as a family.

"We were having such a wonderful time. We were happy and relaxed. Goro and I were both doing well in our respective jobs. He was a banker, and the children were all doing well at school. Life couldn't have felt better…"

While Asa paused, gathering herself, Seagull gently reached out a hand and stroked her silky black hair. The moonlight glistened on the tear gracefully slipping down her cheek. "What happened, Asa?" Seagull feared the answer, but the least she could do was listen.

Asa choked back a sob and the tears fell freely again. "The tsunami," she finally moaned. "The tsunami happened. We were in Sendai, Miyago Prefecture, at the coast. It was about three o'clock in the afternoon. We'd been talking about where we would dine that evening. The wave when it came was so fast, so powerful. I clung to my son and youngest daughter as much as I could. Goro held our eldest daughter tight in his arms." Asa paused, staring into space before continuing. "Our screams were muted by the whooshing sound of gallons of sea water racing towards us. *Don't let go of her!* I cried out to Goro, just as I saw him and my precious girl sucked out to sea."

Seagull felt tears welling in her eyes. *This poor woman.*

Asa nodded to herself. "I frantically tried to keep my head above the water. My little girl was wailing in terror and my son was flailing about, his body tossed up and down by huge waves. I was still close to them. We were all in complete shock."

"Of course you were," Seagull murmured, trying to console Asa, but Asa didn't seem to hear.

Her voice rose. "I don't know what hit me, a falling tree, a kitchen appliance? I just remember coming-to on the shore, surrounded by so much debris and bodies. So many bodies.

"I crawled on my stomach, too weak to stand, my head pounding from whatever'd hit me.

"I desperately searched for my family, my stomach turning at every dead face I saw.

"But they were gone. Just like that, my family was no more. I lay on the shore, hoping nobody would find me. I too wanted to die."

Seagull couldn't stop shaking as she listened to Asa's sad voice. Suddenly, it became clear to her. She had to ask the question, though she already knew the answer. "What were their names? Your son and youngest daughter?"

Asa smiled sadly, fingering the little locket around her throat. "Akira," she whispered, "Akira and Emiko."

Yes, Seagull nodded with a little smile, suddenly, finally understanding the purpose of those ten yen coins.

Twenty-six: Jane

It wasn't the first time Jane had wished Spencer dead, but that was because of his womanizing and disrespect of her. This time the son-of-a-bitch had sent her a card saying how much he missed her. The picture on the card was of a damn bouquet of red roses, and Spencer had inscribed the card to say he'd have real roses, wine, and a big dinner ready for Jane and wanted her home. He loved her, he said.

Well, she didn't love him. In fact she couldn't get Fumio out of her mind. He was the perfect gentleman, and after feeling such a fool for bringing him a gift for the wife he didn't have, he had made Jane feel very much at ease. She didn't even need to drink much anymore to settle her nerves.

Now, even though her working day was over and she was back at the rental, she could see his liquid eyes, sense his presence and smell his earthy scent. Jane was unable to stop wishing she was free and able to pursue a relationship with him. His hand had brushed hers once when he was showing her their automatic pipette instrument, and she could have sworn there were sparks between them. She wanted to pick up the phone and invite him to this grimy flat. But that would be so foolish. He was a colleague. She was a guest in his country and would be going back to the States soon. Tempted though Jane was to prolong the need to stay for the work, she had already planned a course of testing that would readily give him the results he needed to proceed with his research.

Jane picked up the phone and punched in John's number. His latest text had been weird—something about another lost child called Emiko. He must be losing it. He'd better be taking good care of her grandson, Lucas.

John's voice came on. "Mom, where have you been?"

She didn't like the accusation in his tone. She was not his father, full of lies. "Have you found your wife yet? And how is Lucas?"

"The baby's fine. A little sniffly and grumpy but who can blame him? He's probably as exhausted as I am."

Jane noticed he had not asked if she was okay. She felt her spine stiffen. "Where are you staying?"

"Since you made yourself scarce, I ended up in a seedy hotel. But now I'm at the apartment of the guys where Seagull was hiding out. She's gone though and they don't know where."

"Listen, John," Jane's voice was testy. "I am tired of being your nursemaid. You are a grown man. I'm not responsible to pay your bills or wipe your ass."

There was a stony silence. "Mother," at last John spoke, "you have suffocated me for years. I have never asked you for anything. You have imposed yourself, your money, and your opinions upon me. Maybe it's time you stopped." He hung up.

When Jane tried hitting the redial, the phone rang but John didn't answer. You'd think he'd have some concern for his mother. For all he knew she'd been kidnapped for ransom. Not that they did that in Japan. He had no right to be so angry with her as if she were the one that had caused his wife-bitch to desert him.

An hour later, Jane was in a nearby bar, dining on a plate of rice with some sort of shrimp sauce and sipping on hot sake wine. She wasn't crazy about it, but it warmed her stomach which felt like lead. Damn, she felt contaminated and thought she might be about to throw up. The stress would be the death of her! She hoped the pain in her back wasn't a sign of a heart attack. She checked her pulse. It was normal, but Jane was sure her blood pressure must be way higher than it ought to be.

She had done her best to be a good mother and grandmother. She'd even been willing to raise Lucas. She didn't deserve John's recriminations. But a big part of her felt as low as a lab rat because she'd suddenly realized she'd spent her whole life living for her son. As much as Spencer had been an asshole, Jane hadn't really been there for him any more than he was there for her. They'd had nothing more than an arrangement. It was no marriage and she didn't want it anymore. She didn't need him. She was close to hating the man for taking the best years of her life.

Could she file for a divorce from here in Japan? She could ask Fumio about getting an attorney. Probably it would be complicated, but she was damned if she was going to let Spencer off lightly. She'd take half of everything, including his pension.

Jane decided to call Fumio. "Hey," she spoke nervously when he answered. "Sorry to bother you."

"Not at all. How are you?" he sounded polite, his voice gravelly and deep.

"I have a question," she managed to blurt, thinking about divorce attorneys. Was she being a complete fool with a younger, much younger, colleague, who was simply being nice to an older American woman? For all she knew, he might think she was crass and stupid. God damn, she wished she could let go of her insecurity. "I have a question," she repeated.

"I will be happy to help if I can."

"Where..." Jane felt like her heart was about to fail. Her stomach too was doing flip-flops. Now was not the time, but she had to say something. "Where can I learn Japanese?" she croaked.

There was a long pause before Fumio answered. "Ahh," he said and cleared his throat. "Perhaps I can teach you?"

Twenty-seven: John

John cut the call and cursed out loud, ignoring the raised eyebrows of Haruo and the concerned frown of Akira. He was so pissed at his mom! How dare she? What was it with the women in his life, so easily able to make him feel emasculated. First Seagull and now his mom.

Well that was it, he decided, as his cell started ringing and he saw it was Jane again.

Fuck 'em! Both of them!

At least he knew Seagull was alive. If she didn't want him to find her, that was her choice. He was done. John felt mad as hell at her now and it was a good feeling. He had more than proved himself capable of raising Lucas alone, and that's what he decided he would do.

As for his mom, he didn't need her either. Let her drink herself to death for all he cared. He let his cell ring until Jane finally gave up.

He walked over to the makeshift crib where Lucas was sleeping and gazed at his peaceful face. He was so innocent and unaware of the chaos going on around him. John wondered what his son would think when he was older and he told him about their little jaunt to Japan.

He turned to Haruo. "I'm gonna head home tomorrow," he said quietly.

Haruo huffed and Akira shot him an anxious look. "But you can't, you have to help me find Emiko!" the boy yelled.

Haruo suddenly sat up straight. "What?"

As Akira began jabbering in Japanese, John felt suddenly guilty. It was his fault he'd gotten the kid's hopes up about his sister. He should have kept his mouth shut. He wasn't certain the little girl he'd seen back at the hotel even *was* his sister. As far as he knew, she had died in the tsunami.

John was aware of Haruo's eyes upon him, and he knew he was thinking the same. He felt awkward and ashamed as he watched Akira's animated explanation to Haruo. Maybe his mom was right. Maybe he did need to get a backbone.

Torn between taking Lucas home to get some stability back into his short life and helping the young boy in front of him, John knew the best thing to do would be to pack up and go and get on with things, but something was niggling at him.

He realized he was fingering the ten yen coin in his pocket and he made a decision. Something had made him come all this way. What if it wasn't about Seagull after all? What if this was his chance to help somebody else?

Akira looked at him with pleading in his dark eyes.

"Akira?" John's mind was made up. "I'll help you," he said.

Akira lunged at him, his hug nearly knocking him over.

Haruo groaned from the sofa and shook his head as he muttered something in Japanese.

"What did he say?" John asked Akira who was smiling through his happy tears.

He laughed suddenly and Haruo almost smiled too as Akira translated. "He said you're a crazy dude."

Twenty-eight: Seagull

Asa stared at Seagull as she spoke, a strange look on her face.

After Seagull had finished giving her the awesome news about the children, Seagull waited for the joy to appear on Asa's face, a warm hug and amazement at her revelation.

Instead, Asa was silent, her eyes furious, a scowl of contempt on her pale lips. "You sick bitch," she spat.

Seagull, dismayed, recoiled. "What? I--"

Asa jumped up and grabbed Seagull's arm. "Get out of my home!"

Seagull didn't understand. She had just told Asa that she thought her son was alive and she was reacting like this? "Asa, what have I said?"

As Seagull voiced her confusion, Asa began throwing her things into her hold-all. "Out! Out!" Asa was hysterical now and Seagull felt a little scared. "You abandon your child and you think you can repent by making me believe mine is alive?"

"Asa, please calm down," Seagull begged as she stood up, trying to get Asa to look at her.

Asa was sobbing now, tears and mucus running off her chin. She looked like a wild animal, desperate to flee but prepared to fight.

"He may not be *your* Akira. But what if he is?" Seagull dared to ask.

Though Asa's body trembled with rage, Seagull noticed her shoulders visibly relaxing and she continued: "Look, he is the right age, he was adopted by an old monk following the tsunami and now living with another adopted father here in Tokyo."

Asa sank back onto the bed and let Seagull go on.

"Don't you see why I had to tell you? I don't want to get your hopes up unnecessarily but come on, we're intelligent women. We know that there's a chance he is your son."

Asa nodded slowly and looked at her. "You do not know nor understand grief as I have suffered. What I have had to go through in laying my family to rest." Asa's voice trembled.

Seagull tried to put her arm around her shoulder but she pushed it away.

"There have been, and still are, days when I don't want to wake up. Nights when my sleep has been full of dreams of my family, followed by the stark realization that hits me upon waking then the grieving process all over again. I don't know if I can physically, let alone mentally, go through any more loss if this boy is not my son."

Seagull suddenly understood her earlier anger. The thought that maybe a part of her family was still alive must have been overwhelming.

"I know," Seagull said simply.

Asa's response hurt. "No," she sighed, "you don't."

All of a sudden, Seagull thought of Lucas and her breasts began to ache. *Shit! What have I done?* "Oh God," Seagull muttered more to herself than Asa, "I actually think I do."

Twenty-nine: Seagull

Nothing Seagull could say or do would make Asa budge. She had cried and screamed then in the coldest voice she'd announced she had to go to work. And when she got back she wanted Seagull gone. Akira, she had informed Seagull, was an extremely common name. Furthermore, she had been in touch with numerous agencies trying to find him and his little sister. She'd been to all the hospitals for miles and miles around; she'd left photos of her children and her husband with contact information. No one had ever called. There had been no trace.

Seagull wondered at her lack of emotion about *her* family. How had *she* walked away so easily? There must be something seriously wrong with her.

Deciding to take a chance, Seagull called her sister, but she didn't answer her phone and Seagull didn't leave a message. She'd probably be yelled at and made to feel even more miserable anyway.

Seagull realized she was hoping for someone to support her and tell her she was a good person. She was. But now she was also a runaway mother who'd left her family and her medical practice.

She decided she shouldn't dwell on these failings, if that's what they were, right now. She may not have been sure of the rightness of what she'd done, but she couldn't undo her past choices.

Instead she forced herself to concentrate on Asa.

Since Seagull couldn't persuade Asa to take a chance and go see for herself, she decided she'd go back and take a photo of Akira to show the woman. She loved the little boy. She just hoped he didn't hate her. She imagined Haruo giving her the cold shoulder and casting her out of his house.

But she had nothing to lose now. She had nowhere else to go, and she so wanted to make things right for Asa and her family. If Akira *was* Asa's son, somehow Seagull would feel better about herself, Asa was right, but even if he wasn't her child, it seemed better to know the truth.

Would it really dig up Asa's grief? She had heard that people who didn't get the chance to see the bodies of their loved ones were left forever in a sort of limbo, always hoping somehow, someway their beloveds might still be alive. She'd recently read about a GI's remains brought back after decades of being missing in action during WWII. His wife was long since remarried with kids and grandkids, but she still wanted to mourn him. His remains were buried in Arlington with full military honors.

As Seagull wandered along a busy highway inhaling car fumes, she felt crushed by the tall skyscrapers on either side of the road. She stopped and stared at Tokyo Medical University.

Tears were streaming down her face. She had to do this for Asa and Akira.

But if Akira did belong to Asa, what would Haruo do? He loved that little boy.

Seagull felt no matter what direction she turned, she was going to cause hurt to someone. She'd never been a quitter though. She'd managed to get through med school and a tough internship in spite of plenty of hardship and opposition. And in the ER Seagull had been the one to tell people their sister or brother, husband or wife had died. She usually went about it by giving them medical details and listening to them, trying to get *their* stories.

Who, she wondered, would give a damn about *her* story?

Was that why she'd become a doctor so she could be a hero to people and not because her mother expected it? Was that why she wanted Akira to be Asa's son—so she would be applauded? Seagull decided she needed to think this through some more. She walked into the lobby of a nearby hotel which was swank and way too expensive for someone without a job.

After fixing her face in the bathroom, Seagull knew she needed to get back to Akira. However, on an impulse she walked towards the university medical center she'd passed earlier, feeling she had nothing to lose. She was going to march into their human resource department and fill out an application.

But when she got through the doors and saw the young faces of many nationalities, she felt suddenly out of place, out of touch. *I must look such a wreck. Who would hire me?* Clearly, she wasn't thinking straight for she didn't even have a work visa. She was likely to be arrested or deported!

In the nearby lady's room, Seagull examined herself in the mirror, realizing she looked haggard and unprofessional. This was a fool's errand and she felt stupid and worthless. She should have stayed in the States. With a sigh, Seagull went back out to the lobby and sank onto a nearby bench, trying to decide what she ought to do.

Wearily she put her head in her hands, staring down at the floor and suddenly gasped as something caught her eye. There was a ten yen piece on the tile floor. It wasn't the one from Caitlin. That one was safely in her pocket. Yet Seagull felt as if she were about to get a double dose of medicine.

Seagull didn't see *her* at first but she heard *her* voice when the nearby elevator doors opened. Jane! Was she going mad? Seagull contemplated fleeing from the building, but she was tired of running. She walked over to the elevator just as the doors closed. It *was* her! Jane was wearing a white lab coat and talking enthusiastically to a Japanese man, also in a lab coat. She didn't notice Seagull, she was too animated by her companion, who was smiling at her. The elevator stopped at the eleventh floor. And Seagull waited for it to come back then pressed the *up* button.

Wandering along a sterile-looking hallway with labs on either side, Seagull could smell the chemicals. She looked through the windows in each of the doors and finally saw them. They were head to head like co-conspirators staring into a petri dish. She rattled the door so they'd notice her, stepped inside and leant against a workbench. Neither one of them looked up. "Jane," Seagull muttered.

Jane's hand flew up and she stared at Seagull as if she were a dangerous animal. "What the hell are you doing here, Seagull?" she demanded. Her companion looked from Jane to Seagull and back to Jane, his eyes confused.

For some reason, Seagull had expected Jane would politely introduce them. She hadn't expected her tirade.

"Seagull," Jane murmured, her voice dead calm, "you have no business being here. Not only have you deserted my son and *your* baby, but you've managed to cause your poor mother to slash her wrists. Or was it pills she took? I hope you are thoroughly ashamed of yourself. If you expect me to help you, you are mistaken. You can work out this mess for yourself. And so can John. You do know he's in Tokyo, don't you, with Lucas? Not that you'd care..."

"I know," Seagull replied. "Jane, you may not believe this, but there's a reason we are all here in Tokyo."

"Yes, I am here to work." Jane raised her eyebrows, her eyes flashing.

She'd had her hair done, Seagull noticed, and she'd also had a manicure. Her nails were painted bright red. She looked younger, almost pretty. "Did you get a ten yen coin?" Seagull asked, feeling sure she had.

"What are you talking about?" Jane's eyes grew even tenser.

"There's a little boy Akira who might be the missing child of a woman I was staying with. I can't explain all the details. We are here to reunite them."

Thirty: John

John regretted going back to the hotel. The little girl who he suspected might be Akira's sister would be long gone by now.

He had to try though. He'd promised Akira. Haruo too seemed keen to find out if the little girl was Emiko. John felt frustrated at not being able to explain to Haruo his concerns that she was possibly in danger of being prostituted, but there was no way he could get Akira to translate *that!*

Haruo stayed home with Lucas for the day so John could search for Emiko. As he ordered a cola at the bar, John looked around. There were a lot of western businessmen dotted throughout the lounge area. In the lobby he could see a group of elderly Japanese women checking in.

Muttering his thanks to the bartender, he handed over some money. He was fast running out of cash, but Haruo had told him (through Akira) that he didn't need to pay rent, so at least that was covered.

John was hoping he wouldn't be here for too much longer anyway.

As he sipped his drink, he saw her.

She came out of the ladies room, dragging her hands through her hair. She looked tired but still so beautiful.

"Sea!" He called her name as he slammed his glass onto the bar and followed her. She walked out of the door and John gave chase.

He didn't notice the briefcase beside the table until he'd tripped over it, knocking drinks and little pots of wasabi nuts all over the floor. "I'm sorry!" He held up his hands at the angry overweight business man who was wiping spilt tea off his trouser leg.

"Look where you're going arsehole!" John noticed his English accent and apologized once again, all the time thinking Seagull would be well away by now.

Grabbing the last bunch of yen notes from his pocket, John thrust them towards the English man. "Here, for the damage." He was itching to get out of there and back after Seagull, but the man seemed in no rush to let him go.

"As if that will cover it, idiot!" he growled.

A waitress appeared and began to right the table and pick up the spilled mess. "Just accident, sir." The pretty waitress placed a calming hand on the man's arm and he visibly relaxed a little.

"It was. I'm really sorry. I have to go." John heard the man shout something smart as he walked away but ignored him. He needed to catch up with Seagull.

When he got outside though, he knew it was useless. The street was bustling with tourists and locals going about their day to day business.

John looked up and down the street, trying to catch a glimpse of his wife, but he couldn't see her.

"Hey, you!"

John sighed as he heard the English accent behind him and turned to see the man from the hotel bar.

"Man, I've said I'm sorry." He held his hands out as he walked towards the steps of the hotel where the man stood.

"Twenty yen is not going to cover my dry cleaning bill!"

John was pissed now. What *was* this guy's problem? "It's all I have," he emptied his pockets to show him and a ten yen coin dropped to the floor.

"I'll take that too then." The man smiled sinisterly as he crouched down to pick up the coin.

"What? No!" John pushed him as he too bent down to get the coin and the man fell onto his back with a startled groan.

"You fucking..." As the man hastily scrabbled to his feet, John shoved the coin back in his pocket and ran.

A quick glance behind him confirmed the man had given chase. John couldn't help but groan as he darted across the busy road. As John ran through the paved seating area by a huge fountain, the English man continued to chase him, shouting obscenities as passers-by looked on with startled interest.

"John?" Suddenly he heard his mom's voice and looked over towards the bench that it had come from.

His mom was with Seagull! *What the…?*

"I'll call you," John shouted to his mom as he saw the man gaining on him. "Gotta run!"

Leaving his mom and Seagull staring open-mouthed, he laughed to himself as he sprinted off. Checking over his shoulder, John could see the man had slowed and was gasping for breath. Ha, it was probably the most exercise he'd had in years.

John realized he wasn't too far from Haruo's, so he slowed his pace down and began to walk along the shabby streets. A little group of street urchins were playing ball with an old cola can. They were giggling as they kicked it to each other and it made John feel sad that in this day and age, such poverty still existed.

As he went to cross the street, one of the children called out something to John in Japanese. This raised huge amounts of laughter from the other kids so John assumed they were making fun of him, the tall, gangly westerner. He ignored them.

Something made John look back though and that's when he saw Emiko. And he was sure it was Emiko because she was the spit of Akira but with long straggly hair.

"Emiko?" He called out and the little girl looked up whilst the other children continued to stare.

Just as John turned to walk towards them, a thin man came out of a nearby building. He shouted something in Japanese at the kids, and John noticed the instant fear in their faces as he beckoned them angrily.

"Wait!" John shouted but they were filing back into the building behind the man. John was positive it was the same man who had offered him Emiko's services back at the hotel that day.

John knew better than to follow. It was too dangerous, but at least he had seen her and he now knew where to bring the police.

Thirty-one: John

"Mom, Sea," John said, walking back towards them. Sea stopped dead in the street, but his mom kept on coming briskly towards him. She looked weird with a new hairdo and more makeup than he'd ever seen her wearing. As for Sea, he could hardly stand to look at her. Part of him wanted to yell at her, and part of him wanted to hug her. He did neither.

"Just what is going on?" Jane was frowning, looking furious.

John cringed inside but he refused to let her bully him or lead him by the nose ever again. "I could ask you the same but there's no time." He quickly explained about Emiko and how she might be Akira's little sister. "When I said her name, she seemed to recognize it, but then they got scared and all ran inside at the command of this old guy. He looks grandfatherly, but I don't imagine any child would get as scared as they did if he were a decent guy. There's definitely something amiss."

Sea's face was grim, her eyes flashing, but when she caught John looking at her, she looked down. She damn well ought to be ashamed, but he said nothing. What could he say when they had a more pressing matter at hand. "Let's call the police," John said. "We can stand outside somewhere and keep an eye on the door to make sure they don't escape."

Seagull nodded but there was a glint in her eye he didn't like. He knew how bold she could be on occasion, although during her pregnancy and after Lucas' birth, she'd seemed subdued, cowed almost.

The three of them marched back to the house and he pointed out the entrance. "We need to get a translator. We need to call the police."

Jane nodded. "I'll call my colleague, Fumio. He speaks fluent Japanese and English. He'll help."

"What if there's a back door?" Sea asked. "Someone needs to block that until the police get here. Why don't you go round, John, and find out."

John couldn't help but wonder if she planned to run off again.

Seagull read his concern and said, "Don't worry, I'm not going anywhere." Her eyelids half-closed then she opened them wide. "Dirty creep," she muttered.

John had just headed behind the buildings when he heard his mom yelling. He rushed back in time to watch Sea bashing on the door, screaming her head off, demanding they open up. Jane was trying to drag her away. No one came to the door, but he saw a face in an upper window duck out of sight.

He wrapped his arms around Sea and held her tight. She was trembling.

"I am so sorry," she said. "No little girl should be trapped and forced to do god knows what." She moaned, slipped out of John's arms, and collapsed onto the sidewalk. "No child should be abandoned," she cried and began to sob.

"Pull yourself together, Seagull," Jane said sternly, and for once, John was glad of her bossiness. "We don't need you to make a spectacle of yourself. As it is, you've probably alerted these creeps. For all we know, they'll take the kids out the back or worse, they might kill them."

Seagull looked up with horror, her eyes glittering with tears. "No," she said. "No." She pointed down the road. "We've got to keep him out of this. He's just a little boy."

John turned to see Akira coming home from school. There was no way to prevent him from knowing what was happening. They'd need him to call the police and get them to come here. Fast. "Akira, the little girl I saw who looks like you is in this building. We want you to call the authorities--"

Akira's eyes grew big and he rushed up to the door. "Emiko!" he yelled. "Emiko. It's me, your brother. Emiko, open up!"

The door flew open and a man who looked like a sumo wrestler stepped out and shoved Akira onto the ground. Next thing a limo had pulled up and before anyone could stop them, the old grandfather emerged holding the little girl's hand. She didn't look at any of them but obediently got into the car. Several other children were shepherded out and also loaded into the car.

As it rolled away, John could see some numbers on the license plate, but couldn't read the Japanese. He yelled to Akira to try to get the license number.

Everything happened so fast. John's heart was pounding, and his palms were sweating. He wanted to chase the car, but it was already disappearing around the corner. They stood there, all of them, staring helplessly after it, listening to the hum of its engine get more and more distant.

When a small blue car cruised down the road, John waved it over, planning to commandeer it and try to follow the limo, but after it stopped, a tiny Japanese woman with glossy black hair jumped out. She ran towards them. "Akira," she cried.

The boy turned towards her. "Yes," he said, staring at her. "Who are you?"

"Oh, Asa," Sea said. "I am so sorry."

Both Asa and Akira were in tears. "She wasn't my sister," he said. He took a notepad and pen out of his backpack and scribbled something down. "Here," he said, thrusting a piece of paper towards John. "Here is the license plate number. Those kids are in trouble. You go help them."

Thirty-two: Seagull

Seagull held a sobbing Asa in her arms. *What had she done? How could her well-intentioned thinking have been so off-base?* She should never have gotten Asa's hopes up.

John and Jane looked at her questioningly. She quickly explained to them how she'd thought and hoped Akira was her lost son. She glanced down and realized Akira was listening intently as she spoke. John put a comforting arm around the little boy's shoulders. Once again, Seagull felt less than useless. *Who was she to meddle in other people's grief and loss? She'd abandoned her child and now she'd caused more hurt in the lives of these strangers.*

Asa freed herself from Seagull's hug and spoke softly to Akira, crouching down a little to make eye contact. "What happened to you and your family, Akira?"

Akira replied in Japanese to Asa. Her eyes grew even cloudier. She couldn't stop crying softly throughout his tragic tale, nodding every now and again, and sometimes shaking her head sadly.

Finally, when he stopped talking, she took hold of his arms and whispered softly, this time in English. "But you have a home now, a family?"

Akira nodded and a brief flicker of a smile crossed his young face as he no doubt thought of Haruo.

Asa smiled back. "Good," she said simply, letting go of the boy and standing up. She wiped her eyes. "I'm tired. I'm going home." She looked towards Seagull.

Seagull met her eyes. "I'll come too." She shivered inside, expecting to be rudely rejected, but Asa, who seemed softer towards her, was shaking her head, a sympathetic smile on her face.

"I think you have unfinished business." Asa nodded her head towards John.

Seagull felt the shame begin to glow on her face.

John looked awkwardly to the floor, and even Jane had the decency to look away.

At last John cleared his throat. "First and foremost, we need to contact the police and give them that license plate, okay?"

Akira nodded in agreement and Jane muttered her yes.

"I can do that if you wish?" Asa offered.

Akira passed her the slip of paper he had been gripping.

"Thank you," Asa bent down to kiss his cheek, "and good luck, Akira."

Akira blushed slightly, watching Asa walk back to her car.

Seagull knew Asa was right. She did have unfinished business. Asa had lost her husband and her kids, whereas she still had a husband and a child. She owed John an explanation, and she needed to see her baby. Her breasts ached at the thought. She stepped towards John. "Can I come back with you so that we can talk for a while?" she asked, dreading his response.

John looked at her coldly for a few long seconds before replying. "Seagull, a few days ago, I would have given anything to hear you say that." He stopped talking and his hand shook slightly as he ran it through his hair, a nervous habit Seagull knew only too well. She knew there was a *but* coming and felt hollow inside.

"John, you *do* need to talk."

There was Jane again, interrupting as usual, though this time Seagull was grateful and flashed a smile of thanks at her.

"Argh!" John groaned and kicked the wall.

They all cringed. Akira, wide-eyed, stepped back.

"Will you all just stop telling me what I need, what I want!" John glared at Seagull.

She couldn't help but see the raw pain in his eyes. She'd hurt him so badly and he'd never deserved that. He'd always treated her with love and kindness. He'd always encouraged her endeavors. He'd been her biggest cheer-leader. Whatever her feelings towards him and Lucas, and she still didn't know what they were, she had gone about this completely the wrong way. "John," she stepped towards him. Despite his rage, she knew he would never hurt her. She had always known that. "I have fucked up on a huge scale." She ignored John's harrumph and continued, "But I need to explain, if I can, why I did what I did."

Another car pulled up beside them, this time a silver Mercedes. Jane waved. "Here's my ride," she said gaily.

Seagull noticed the brightness in her eyes and the slight flush across her neck and chest. *Well, well, well, this is interesting.* She wondered if John had noticed it too. If he did, he said nothing.

Fumio, the guy Jane was with earlier stepped out of the car and came towards them.

Jane's voice shook slightly when she began introducing them. "John…"

Seagull raised her eyebrows in amusement. The woman clearly fancied the guy and was frightened of what her son might think. Seagull felt instantly mean to find her mother-in-law's discomfort funny.

Jane, her eyes glued on John, swallowed hard. "This is Fumio, my boss."

John clearly didn't get it. He shook Fumio's hand and made polite talk.

All of a sudden, Jane threw her hands out in a gesture of understanding. "Asa!" Everyone looked at her in surprise. "Of course!" she exclaimed as she gently batted her forehead.

Fumio frowned. "My sister, Asa?"

"Yes! She was just here. Seagull's been staying with her."

"She's *your* sister?" Seagull looked at Fumio who looked back at her non-committedly.

He listened intently while Jane explained to him what'd brought Asa here today, his eyes looking stormier with every word. He fixed a frown upon Seagull.

Jesus, this man was pissed at her.

Way to go Seagull!

"How dare you?" He glared at Seagull. "How dare you put my sister through this mess?"

"I'm sorry," Seagull stammered, but he'd already turned away from her.

"Can I drop you somewhere?" Fumio offered to John who was already shaking his head, looking at Seagull then to Akira. "No, thanks, but we'll walk. We're just around the corner."

With a final cursory glare at Seagull, Fumio strode to his car with Jane not far behind. She gave Seagull one of her famous "I told you so" looks and got in the car next to Fumio, telling John she'd call him later.

As the Mercedes sped up the street, John and Seagull cautiously met one another's eyes.

It seemed a long time before they heard a little cough beside them from Akira.

"Okay," John muttered, "let's go." He and Akira began to walk away while Seagull stood watching, sadness filling her entire being.

She stared helplessly at the ground and wiped a lone tear from her face.

"Well?" John stopped.

She shrugged her shoulders, not knowing what to say.

"What are you waiting for? Come on!"

She couldn't help but smile her relief as she hurried to catch up with them and she couldn't help but notice Akira was smiling too.

Thirty-three: Akira

"It isn't about Nishimachi," Akira said in Japanese to Haruo who grunted and ignored him, chopping an onion with heavy handed thumps. "I learn English without going to school."

John, who was sitting at the table, got a puzzled expression, obviously not understanding much of what'd transpired.

Seagull, rocking Lucas, looked up, her eyes red and puffy from crying. She looked at Haruo's irritated face and back to Akira. "What?"

Akira smiled and spoke English to her. "Your baby back, you back, good, but not about you. More to do."

"I know," Seagull said. "I so want Lucas to learn I am his mother." She had tried to get him to breastfeed, but the baby had turned away, and John had to feed him his formula from a disposable bottle.

"No!" Akira said, his voice strong and firm. He took a ten yen coin out of his pocket. "Who else got them?"

"I have one," John said.

"Me too," said Seagull.

Haruo shook his head, muttering something in Japanese to express his frustration at what he clearly thought nonsense. "Ten yen won't buy much rice," he said, this time in English. It sounded as if it were right out of a Japanese/English phrase book.

Akira grinned. "Where you learn English, Haruo? You been reading my books?"

John fished out his ten yen coin from his pocket and put it on the table with a click.

"Yours, please." Akira held his hand out to Seagull.

"Just a minute." Clearly reluctant to put Lucas down or turn him over to John, she carried him over to her purse and managed to get the coin out. She dutifully handed it to Akira, who put it on top of John's before placing his own coin over to one side.

"One more!" he demanded and looked meaningfully at Haruo.

"I don't have one!" Haruo yelled.

"There is one more!" Akira said stubbornly. "Who has it?" his voice went up a little in frustration.

"It must be your mother, John," Seagull said. "Unless it's Asa."

"Asa," Akira said, and he looked up at the ceiling and became silent, thoughtful. "Asa," he said. "Not her. Jane."

"This is weird." John said, an alarmed look on his face. "There's something wrong with this kid."

"Nothing wrong with me." Akira responded. Suddenly he groaned.

Seagull handed Lucas to John, who looked helpless and cradled the baby as much for his own comfort as the child's, before wrapping her arms around Akira. "What, sweetheart? What's the matter?"

"Emiko," he sputtered. "It's my fault."

"Hush," Seagull murmured. "What can possibly be your fault?"

Akira grimaced. "You don't understand."

"I have a sister, my twin, Sarah. She is very angry with me. I left her and didn't tell her. I didn't tell her anything about what I was feeling. I told no one. I'm not even sure… It wasn't because I didn't love her…"

"But I did *not* love Emiko. I wished her dead."

Haruo's face glowered with rage. "Not you," he said. "Tsunami!"

"I caused it!" Akira cried.

The small room became silent. The rice steamed and made it feel hot and humid. Lucas burped and threw up on John. Seagull grabbed a dishcloth and rushed over, fussing and trying to wipe the spit from John's shoulder. "Is he okay?" she asked in a pleading voice.

"It's what babies do," John murmured, kissing the top of Lucas' head. "He's fine."

Seagull squeezed the top of John's arm. "You'll have to teach me."

"We'll see," John said noncommittally but there was a sparkle in his eye.

Haruo slammed his fist onto the stove. "Rice and fish ready," he said. "We eat." He turned towards Akira and went over and kneeled next to him and spoke Japanese.

Akira nodded a few times. Finally, he looked up. "We eat dinner. Emiko maybe not dead. Maybe gangster son-of-a-bitch," he paused and grinned at their shocked faces. "I speak good American? Maybe sons-of-bitches," he continued, "need a lesson. Other kids not lucky like me." He grinned at Haruo whose eyes were full of concern for his son. "You better get Jane," he announced. "She one crazy dude."

Thirty-four: Jane

Fumio handed Jane a glass of wine which she gratefully accepted with shaky hands. As she continued to fill him in on all of the day's events, she sank wearily into his sofa.

"Just a minute," he interrupted, and pulled his cell phone out of his shirt pocket. "That damn Seagull woman," he muttered, punching a number into his phone. "She is nothing but trouble."

Jane gripped her wine glass, not knowing what to do or say, but she had the feeling anything she said could be taken the wrong way. He looked horribly upset.

"Damn, she's not picking up!" He cut the call and frowned. "This could destroy my sister!"

Jane let out a sigh of relief. He was upset for Asa, but she'd seemed fairly okay. "Seagull should have minded her own business, but your sister handled things well."

"Asa always seems okay on the outside. She's a doctor trained to not show her feelings." Fumio sank onto the couch next to Jane, leaning forward with his head in his hands. "Don't you see?" He looked up with tears in his eyes. "Asa has been to hell and back after the loss of her family. She very nearly didn't make it herself! So many times I expected a call to tell me she'd taken her own life. *That's* how bad she was!" Fumio shook his head, remembering who knew what scenes he'd witnessed.

Jane placed her hand gently on his arm. "I'm so sorry," she whispered, disliking Seagull even more for the mess she'd caused.

"And it wasn't *her* Akira, you're sure?" His eyes pleaded with Jane's.

Jane met his gaze but soon cast her eyes down. "No, it wasn't her son.

A mother would know." She stroked his arm.

The man looked lost as if he might be about to cry. "And the little girl?"

Jane shrugged. "Asa is going to contact the police and give them the license plate. There's nothing more we can do."

Fumio suddenly jumped up. "I need to be with Asa."

"Wait Fumio, I--"

"Jane, this could well set her back. I need to make sure she's ok."

Jane stood up next to him, resisting the urge to put her arms around him to comfort him. "I understand, Fumio, but look, Seagull is staying with her so--"

Fumio grunted. "Pfft!"

"I know, I know." Jane reached down into her purse for her cell. "Let me call Seagull and see how Asa is, ok?"

Fumio said nothing. Jane took his silence as an assent and dialed Seagull's number.

Seagull sounded crushed.

Jane felt a little sorry for her for some reason. "Seagull, are you with Asa? Have you seen her since earlier?"

Jane heard Seagull begin to sob. *Now what?* Jane wanted to give her daughter-in-law a piece of her mind. As it was, she had a sinking feeling. She glanced up nervously at Fumio. "Seagull, what is it? What's happened?"

Fumio looked about to snatch the phone from her. "What? What's happened?" He repeated her question, her eyes intense.

Jane silenced him with her finger, trying to decipher what Seagull was saying.

"Oh God. Look, we'll be right over okay? Stay with her, Seagull." She hung up and took in Fumio's overwrought behavior, hopping from foot to foot clearly desperate to hear what was going on. Jane cleared her throat, preparing to give him the news scared at how he might react. "Asa contacted the police about the prostituted children."

Fumio nodded impatiently.

"It seems they were onto them already, but it's quite a large and professional group that are doing this."

"Okay. And?"

Jane smarted a little at Fumio's tone but continued nevertheless. "The police had photos taken by their surveillance group which they showed to Asa and Seagull."

"Seagull saw the kids earlier, right?"

"I think so," Jane nodded. "One of the children, a little girl..." she paused, unable to voice the incredible words.

"Yes?"

Jane looked deeply into Fumio's eyes. "The little girl is Emiko, your niece, Asa's daughter."

Thirty-five: Jane

Fumio drove like a maniac, dodging in and out of cars and trucks, his hand constantly on the horn. Jane felt as if she was in the Indie 500. He nearly caused an accident when he ran a red light, but he didn't stop and he didn't look back at the sound of screeching brakes. His eyes stared straight ahead. He was a man who would not be thwarted. His fierceness was turning Jane on which was ridiculous. There was definitely more important business at hand, but just what he intended to do once they got to Asa's place, she had no idea. Actually, the man was a little frightening. His anger was palpable.

He screeched around a taxi and sped into a parking space. After fumbling in the back seat for a small red medical kit, he jumped out of the car, and, surprisingly, headed around the car to open the passenger door for Jane. He was not smiling, but this gesture told her clearly he wanted her by his side. She had no time to worry about *how* or *if* that might blossom into something permanent. There was only *now*.

She hurried with him to Asa's apartment. The door was ajar. They heard raised voices. Fumio marched inside, going directly over to his sister, who was doing her best to escape the grip of Seagull who was hanging onto her wrists. Akira was wrapped around her legs. It was like an intervention from a family trying to control an alcoholic. Jane felt a pang of shame.

Asa saw Fumio. "Brother," she gasped. "Tell them to let me go. I must find her! I must go now!" She stomped her foot. "Let me go," she wailed.

"Asa," Fumio said sternly. "Calm down. We will find Emiko. Trust me." He quickly opened his medical kit and took out a syringe and filled it from a small vial.

Asa cringed and crouched to the floor. "No," she said, sounding utterly defeated. "Not again."

Seagull stroked her head. "Don't worry. We will find Emiko. The police probably know where they've taken the children."

"Wait," Jane said, realizing Fumio planned to sedate his sister, and she knew it. "Wait. Asa is rightfully upset. We need to act together."

"Jane," Fumio hesitated, "I told you she is in a delicate mental state."

Asa sighed deeply. "I lost my entire family. Now I learn my little girl is alive. She's alive! I have to fetch her home. I must!"

Akira hugged Asa. "I wish you were my mother," he said. "You, Jane-lady, you got the coin?"

Jane was thoroughly confused.

John soon enlightened her. "Remember, Mom, the email about the ten yen coins? You did get one, right?"

Suddenly it came back to Jane. Spencer almost finding her bottle of vodka but digging out that odd coin instead. She'd forgotten all about it.

Another Japanese guy, wearing coveralls, with a broad face and dark eyes strode over to Jane. "Coin," he demanded, and held out his hand.

Fumio bristled.

Even though Jane didn't feel threatened, she felt protected.

"Who are you?" Fumio asked angrily.

"I'm Akira's father." The man looked tough, but there was a gentle light in his eyes when he said his son's name.

"Haruo," Asa said, smiling sadly toward him. "You are so lucky to have Akira."

Jane fumbled in her purse and came up with a ten yen piece out of a mess of small change. There were several, but at this moment she suspected it would make no difference.

Akira took the coin and held it in the palm of his hand, eyeing the ceiling. After a few moments, he looked puzzled. "Wrong one," he said.

Jane almost asked what the hell difference a coin could make, but all eyes were on her, and she couldn't be mean to the boy. She tried to remember what she'd done with the coin Spencer had found. Had he kept it? She dumped out the contents of her purse hoping it would surface, but there was only a mismatch of old keys, a couple of dimes, chapstick, and several pens.

"It's probably back in the States," she muttered, feeling as if she'd committed a major faux pas. She wanted to shout at their accusatory faces, *How was I supposed to know what do to with a worthless piece of money?* "What is this about?" she asked instead. "Why is that particular coin so important?"

John answered. "There are four of them. Each person has been selected--"

Jane was about to interrupt to tell him not to be ridiculous, but Fumio shook his head to caution her to be quiet. She managed to keep her opinion to herself. "Go on, John," she said.

While John spoke, Haruo offered Asa his hand and helped her stand. She leaned into him for a while before brushing herself off. "I don't care you think you have all been chosen. You big people can take care of yourselves. My little daughter and other children need help. I know police are involved, but if they wait too long, the kids are going to be murdered or moved where we will never find them. Surely there is something, some way to find out where the children were taken. The police would not say, but I think they know more. I think, too," she looked desperately at each of us, "maybe we can get them out safely."

Fumio put away his syringe, looking thoughtfully toward his sister. "What do you think we ought to do?"

"I am going back to the police station and I am going to demand they tell me where the kids were taken." She spun around, her hands on her slim hips, her eyes piercing everyone's in the room, except for Akira's. "Is anyone coming with me?"

"We will come," Haruo said and took Akira's hand.

Thirty-six: Caitlin

"Good God." Caitlin buried her head in her hands with a loud sigh as Paul looked up from his armchair across the room.

"What's up, babe?"

Caitlin eyed him wearily. "Come read this." She pointed to the laptop screen in front of her and stood up. "I need a drink."

As she strode from the living room, Paul put down the script he'd been reading and went to Caitlin's desk where he sat and began to read.

A few minutes later, Caitlin was back with a large glass of white wine in her hand.

"Well?" She leant against the door frame, her eyebrows raised and a dissatisfied pout on her lips.

Paul looked away from the computer screen towards her. His eyes were incredulous and he was annoyed. "Fuck."

Caitlin snorted, "Fuck indeed." She walked into the room and flopped onto the sofa. "Argh, baby! I thought our part in this was over!"

Paul suddenly stood up and went to her. "Woah, woah, Cait." His hands were raised as if to stop her. "This is nothing to do with us. We've done our bit. We're not getting involved with this. No fucking way!"

"Paul!" Caitlin jumped up quickly and a trickle of wine splashed from her glass onto the carpet. Ignoring it, she looked Paul squarely in the eyes. "We have to do something, Paul." She was firm in her tone.

Paul sighed inwardly knowing how determined his wife could be. "Look Cait, baby, Seagull's email says they're working with the Tokyo police to find those kids. There's nothing we can do."

"But what about that coin, the one Jane got? I should check with her husband, see if it's with him and if so…"

Paul was shaking his head. "Please don't say what I think you're gonna say."

"Paul, you know these coins are special; they are what can help this situation. I need to get the missing one to Tokyo. To Jane."

"Fuck you, Caitlin! You do this, you do it alone. You hear me?" Paul strode from the room.

Caitlin stared open mouthed before chasing after him. "Your child was saved because of those coins! Do you not want other children to be?"

Paul ignored her, walking into the kitchen and standing with his back to her.

Caitlin could see the tension in his shoulders, and it reminded her of a time, way before they got together, when she'd had to impart bad news to him. It had been a different house, a different situation, but it was the same rage that flooded his body now and she wondered why. Gently, she placed a hand on the back of his neck, rubbing it with her thumb and forefinger as she finally felt him begin to relax under her touch. "Baby," she whispered as she leant into his back. "What's up?"

Paul turned to her, his hands around her waist. "It scares me, Cait." He shook his head. "I don't know, just the power of these coins. It scares me."

Caitlin nodded as she leant her head on his shoulder; "They've only ever done good baby."

Paul sighed but said nothing.

"We've both been given so much from those little coins. Is it not our duty to make sure they are allowed to continue their work and help others?" Her husband's continued silence confirmed to Caitlin that he couldn't disagree. She hugged him tight **and,** kissing his cheek, she whispered, "I'll contact Jane's husband now."

As she walked from the kitchen, Paul stared after her, shaking his head wearily.

Thirty-seven: Jane

"Hush, Lucas, honey," Jane murmured, as she rocked the baby in her arms. At last, after having walked him around Haruo's tiny apartment for twenty minutes almost tripping over furniture and belongings, Lucas fell asleep. With relief, Jane placed him on the pile of towels Haruo had made for his bed. She was so angry with her son for bringing his child here in pursuit of Seagull. She was angry too at Seagull for being so damn irresponsible. As for Asa, she completely understood her reckless need to storm the police station and make them tell her where the kidnapped children were being held. Though Jane was pretty sure they wouldn't reveal anything.

Despite her disdain for the gritty little room which could use a damn good cleaning and disinfecting, Jane was relieved Haruo and Akira hadn't stayed. She needed to be alone. She felt terrible that she hadn't been able to produce the ten yen piece they seemed to think had magical properties. For sure, Fumio did not believe such nonsense, but he'd gone to the police station with his sister Asa to steady her. Jane thought Haruo would be the best one for that job. He'd hopped into the front seat with Asa in quite a hurry, leaving Fumio and Akira to follow behind her little car.

Jane wished Akira hadn't been so distraught about the coin. His big eyes had filled with tears when she'd told him it must be back in the States. He'd insisted on getting it as soon as possible, and Seagull had emailed some woman, Caitlin. Apparently, she'd been the one to alert John of Sea's whereabouts. Jane wished she'd minded her own business.

Suddenly it dawned on her. All they needed to do was have the coin express-mailed to Tokyo. It could be there as early as tomorrow morning.

With shaking hands, Jane dialed Spencer's cell. She really did *not*

122

want to talk to him. She needed a drink, but there was nothing in this place, not even a beer.

His baritone voice answered. "Jane, thank Christ. When are you coming home?"

"I don't know yet," Jane hedged. "I called about something else."

"What?" he sounded irritated.

In the past, Jane had always capitulated to Spencer's moods and tried to placate him whilst drinking herself silly. Not this time. "Spencer, I need for you to get that ten yen coin you found in my purse and express mail it to me here in Tokyo."

"Why don't you come get it yourself?" he replied testily. "I miss you. I want you home."

"What for? To cook dinners you never show up on time for? To clean the house? Hot sex?" Jane's voice sounded bitter, even to her.

There was a silence at the end of the line.

"Spencer, this is important to me."

"Did you get my card?"

"Yes, it was lovely," she lied, aware her voice had gone up an octave, remembering how she had thrown it in the trash can.

A wave of emotion suddenly took hold of her. She felt incredibly sad and lonely as she remembered the diapers she'd changed by herself for years and all those solitary times she'd attended John's childhood events. She remembered the yearning for a sense of purpose greater than doing her best to be a good mother. Remembered how much she'd hated to be Spencer's wife.

"I'm not coming home, Spencer."

An image of her luxurious house flashed into Jane's mind—so much more comfortable than this dump, but at what cost? Why on earth should she stay married to this man? He certainly didn't find her enough of a woman to satisfy his lusts. "Look for the coin, would you? It's probably on the kitchen counter."

"Are you ever planning on coming home?" Spencer's voice was measured almost as if he were holding his breath.

"I don't know," she answered honestly, so tired of the lies between them.

"If you leave me," he said, "I'll not give you a penny in alimony or support. You will find yourself on the street with your bottles of vodka running dry."

Jane was stunned. "You're the one drove me to drink," she muttered.

"Come on!" he responded. "No one put a gun to your head to marry me. No one told you to dote on our son to the detriment of any relationship between you and I."

Jane realized Spencer was right. She *had* shut him out after the birth of John. But what woman doesn't put her child first? It was way too late for this conversation. "I cannot come home right now. It's simply not possible." There was a metallic snapping on the line.

"Hear that? I've got your coin, but the only way you're getting it is to fetch it yourself." Spencer cleared his throat. "You had no business running off to Japan like that without asking me what I thought."

There was no time for arguing with him now, but Jane couldn't contain her frustration after years of anger. "You know what, Spencer. I've had enough of you. Why don't you get one of your tarts in to keep you company unless you've already got one there."

"Go to hell!" he shouted.

She knew he hadn't hung up, but Jane had nothing more to say to Spencer. Not a word. Not a syllable. She calmly hit *end call* and sat for a moment staring at Akira's old computer on the worn table. Without booze, she felt panicky. She needed to keep busy; she had Lucas to think about.

What, what, what, Jane moaned to myself, *am I going to do now?* She hated that she'd let everyone down by stupidly leaving the ten yen coin at home. Or had she? Vaguely, she remembered in the excitement of packing to fly to Tokyo, she'd held the coin in her hand, thanking it for her good luck. Could Spencer be baiting her? It would be so like him.

Fetching her purse and dumping out the contents onto the floor, Jane searched through them again, but no coin appeared. *Hell!*

For the next ten minutes, Jane sat next to Lucas, watching his steady breathing and wishing she could turn back the time so he was her child, not her grandchild. She would change so many things. For one thing she wouldn't have married Spencer, she'd have raised John on her own. When had she become so dependent, needing a man's income to support her? Why hadn't she pursued the career she'd wanted rather than putting everyone else first? It was what was expected of her and most women at that time, but things had changed for the better for women. Seagull was an example of that reality. For once Jane found she didn't wish Seagull dead. She must have been so confused to have run away from her child and from John. Jane knew Seagull was suffering a lot of guilt, and she actually did love John. When they'd both gotten in Asa's car, Jane had noticed them leaning against one another.

Poor Asa, her face had been so pale. Beneath her jet-black hair, she'd looked like a beautiful ghost. That's how Jane had felt in her marriage for so long, she mused now—invisible. If she divorced Spencer, would life be any better with Fumio or was she dreaming of something impossible and unrealistic? Maybe he was just being kind to an older woman and had no romantic notions. What if she ended up alone?

The thought of hurting Spencer, in spite of everything, chilled her. They had a history together. They were a family. It must be a terrible thing to lose the husband you love and your kids. Christ, Jane hoped they got Asa's daughter back. If only there was something more she could do. Baby-sitting wasn't enough. Of course it never was.

She turned on Akira's computer and hit the Explorer key. The internet popped onto the screen and Jane searched for Tokyo Metropolitan Police then clicked onto their website. Soon, she had accessed their HTML coding. An easy task so far, but Jane had never hacked into anyone's website despite knowing how. If she were successful and these Japanese police kept up-to-date records, she just might discover the whereabouts of Emiko and the other children.

Thirty-eight: Seagull

Seagull felt exhausted. The past few days had been so draining, emotionally.

She was now reunited with her child whilst Asa, still grieving her loss, might soon be reunited with hers. It was such a rollercoaster.

At thoughts of her son, Seagull's breasts began to ache, and she hugged herself at the thought of cradling him again. How strange? For so long she hadn't been able to stand her baby anywhere near her, now she felt like she needed him as much as he needed her, if not more.

Seagull could barely comprehend the bond she seemed to be forming with Lucas, after the first few cold, for her, barren months of his life. She wondered how Jane was coping with him whilst John was at the police station with the others. Should she have gone with them or even stayed with Lucas rather than remain at Asa's place?

Seagull had already emailed Caitlin, but there was something else she needed to do. She flopped onto the guest bed and took out her cell phone. For a few minutes she simply studied the gadget in her hands, turning it over and over, along with the thoughts in her head. She knew she needed to make the call but was dreading it. She'd put it off for as long as possible. With everything that had been going on lately, she just hadn't gotten around to it, though Seagull knew that was a pretty lame excuse.

She was certainly going to get an earful of abuse from her sister, Sarah, who would be furious she'd ran away and left her to deal with the consequences of their mom.

Mom. Seagull sighed as she thought of her mother and the relationship they had. At least she hoped they *did* still have a relationship. But no, surely she would have heard if the worst had happened.

Seagull had always felt such a huge disappointment to her parents. Oh she'd been clever enough and popular amongst her peers, but there was a wild side within her they'd never understood.

The frustration for many years though was they had never *tried* to understand her. In her dad's eyes she was simply *so volatile*, and her mom just thought she was going through a phase. A twenty year phase!

Feeling a sudden surge of repressed anger, Seagull realized she'd spent too much of her life doing what people expected of her instead of what made *her* happy. She knew her parents could hardly believe it when she met and married John, the steadying influence they so desperately craved for her. Was that what her initial attraction to him had been, to prove to her mom and dad she *could* do the right thing?

It was suddenly all clear to her and it felt quite a liberating realization.

She did love John, of course, but for quite a while there hadn't been that passion between them that Seagull craved. In all honesty, she thought, there probably never had been. It struck her as to how very sad their situation was.

She felt she was slowly coming to terms, *finally,* with motherhood and the weight of responsibility that came with it. She would never abandon Lucas again. Her marriage however, that was another matter. Seagull needed to do some soul searching before she made any solid decisions on that.

With a heavy heart, she unlocked her cell and punched in Sarah's number.

Thirty-nine: John

John watched a silent Fumio flooring the accelerator to keep up with his sister, Asa. Her car was nowhere near as fast as his Mercedes, but she was darting in and out of traffic like a pro. At least she was obeying the traffic laws and stopping at red lights, which was more than John could say for Fumio, who was rushing through every intersection, no doubt because he didn't want to lose his sister in the crush of cars.

Sea. Why hadn't he insisted she come? All that crap she'd given about wanting to be alone, needing to make a call to her sister. Why couldn't that have waited? She'd wanted to keep Lucas with her, but John hadn't let her. She must have thought he was a real ass-wipe. Though John wasn't sure if he cared what she thought about him anymore. He was done chasing her the way he had in their college days. Not to mention this crazy fucking journey across the world with his baby son in tow. Jeez, what affect had any of this had on Lucas? John only hoped it was helping him at some level to know he was loved, and he could go anywhere and do anything without fear.

As for his mom, she was no better than Seagull, rushing over to Japan, dumping his dad and him for her so-called work. She'd been harping on for years about John and his dad preventing her from fulfilling her life's ambition. But from what he could see, her life's work was currently about giving Fumio the eye. He was a good looking man and a smart intellectual like her, but years younger. Though John had to admit, the reason he'd insisted on Jane keeping Lucas with her was because he was getting a vibe of sparks flying between Fumio and his mother. His mother! Christ, he damn well intended to stop that bullshit from happening.

"I appreciate you dropping Jane off at Haruo's," John said, glancing at

Fumio behind the wheel.

Fumio grunted and nodded. "No problem."

John suddenly felt the need to explain. "Lucas's diapers and formula are there."

"I get it," Fumio replied. "Lucas is in good care with Jane."

John noticed how his voice softened when he said Jane and it irritated him.

John decided to change the subject. "I don't blame Asa for wanting to confront the cops."

Fumio drummed the steering wheel with his fingers and glanced sideways at him.

John sighed heavily. "I just hope she won't be hurt more. They're unlikely to release any information to us. We'll probably be labeled vigilantes."

Fumio nodded his head. "Keishichō." He caught up with his sister's car, which she was expertly backing into a parking spot outside a tall wedge-shaped building. "Metropolitan Police building," he added, probably for John's benefit, swerving up a side street in search of parking.

There was construction blocking the other side of the road, and they were forced to wait. John could sense Fumio's impatience. "You know, Haruo is a good guy. She'll be all right," John said.

Fumio remained silent. At last they were waved on by a road worker and managed to locate a pay and display parking area. Fumio got a ticket and put it on the dashboard before marching ahead of John into the building.

Once inside, John felt helpless, staring at the Japanese directory on the wall next to the elevators. The only things he understood were floor numbers. Fumio punched the up button. "Where are we going?" John asked, as the elevator doors slid open.

"Criminal Investigation," Fumio answered, bowing slightly to the people getting off the elevator. "Needle in a haystack," he muttered and rolled his eyes.

They followed signs to an office where a middle-aged woman was sitting behind a safety shield. Her black hair was turning gray, but she had a streak of blond sweeping across her forehead. There was no sign of Asa and the others. Fumio spoke to the woman, nodding his head. "Yes, we will try there. Thank you," he said in English, perhaps realizing just how completely in the dark John felt.

John couldn't help but respect this man. "Where?" he asked, wanting to help and not be a fifth wheel. He was beginning to wish he had stayed home with Lucas, but the thought of Fumio leading his mother down any hallway made his stomach churn.

"There is department called Organized Crime Control. It is our best hope."

The moment they stepped out of the elevator, they could hear Asa's raised voice. Fumio sprinted towards the sound with John not far behind. Asa might have been diminutive in size, but she had three officers, all much taller than her, cowed. Haruo was standing protectively behind her, holding Akira's hand.

She yelled at them in a torrent of Japanese and stamped her feet. Akira, apparently seeing she was about to throw herself onto one of the nearest officers, grabbed Asa's hand. She seemed to calm down. She shook her head as Haruo put his arm around her shoulder and led her away. Fumio spoke a few words to the officers, who nodded with understanding in their eyes.

"Tea?" John suggested weakly, noticing a sign of a square white plate, delicate rice dishes, and chopsticks which he assumed indicated the presence of a cafeteria. He felt suddenly exhausted and needed to sit and gather himself. He was missing Lucas and dare he say it, Seagull.

His heart lurched. Could hearts lurch? What did that mean? To John it meant he wanted to share this moment, share an exotic meal in a foreign cafeteria with the woman he loved. And even if it was a bust, the tea like vinegar, and sushi which he hated, he wanted them, him and Sea, to be able to sip saké or tea or whatever and laugh their heads off, hugging their little boy, promising to work on their relationship. Especially Sea. Suddenly, John's forehead was beaded with perspiration. Maybe he wasn't so lily-white either.

Forty: Caitlin

Caitlin felt an instant dislike to the man who opened the door to her. "Spencer?"

"Who's asking?" He smirked, looking her up and down and making the hairs on the back of her neck stand up and her stomach heave with nausea.

Gathering herself, Caitlin stuck her hand out, her business-like demeanor kicking in again. "Caitlin Somerville. I'm here about the coin." She waited whilst he sized her up before finally shaking her hand and stepping aside for her to enter the house.

"Ah yes, the coin." Spencer chortled as he closed the door behind her and led Caitlin into the living room.

Resisting the urge to ask him what was so funny, Caitlin sat in the chair he gestured towards and crossed her legs.

"So tell me," Spencer gazed longingly at her legs, and Caitlin pulled her skirt over her knees, regretting not having worn trousers.

"What is it about this, erm, mysterious coin?" Again, that little chortle as if he were humoring her.

She wished she could slap his smug face. "It's difficult to understand..."

Spencer interrupted her. "I do love an English accent. Drink?" He stood and poured himself a large measure of whiskey from the decanter on the coffee table in the center of the room. "Care for one?"

"No thanks," Caitlin said, a little annoyed. Did he think this was a social visit? "The coins really do have some sort of power. I have witnessed it first hand, twice."

Spencer did not even bother to smother his laughter.

Caitlin stood up. "Look, if you don't mind, just give me your wife's coin and I'll be gone."

"Oh dear, I'm sorry, I seem to have offended you." Spencer looked suitably shame-faced. "Please, go on."

Caitlin sat back down and spoke adamantly.

After she'd finished talking, Spencer looked thoughtful. "So you think Jane was given the coin to help these Japanese children?"

Caitlin shrugged, glad she finally had his attention and he was taking her seriously. "Who knows, she may have received it for another reason. The point is, she needs it now. If it *can* help those children, surely it's worth a try?"

Spencer nodded and stared at the floor for a few uncomfortable moments as Caitlin shifted awkwardly in the stiff armchair.

"I have reservations, Mrs. Somerville."

Caitlin raised her eyebrows questioningly and waited as Spencer took a deep breath.

"What if the coin is about Jane?"

Caitlin said nothing, allowing him to continue.

"I..." Spencer gulped, and suddenly Caitlin could see he wasn't the brash over-confident man she had initially thought. "I love my wife but I haven't always been a very good husband to her." Spencer slugged back his drink and slammed the glass on the table. "What if this coin is to free Jane? From me. What if she never comes back?"

Caitlin leant forward, a sympathetic smile on her face. "I hope you two can work things out. But we can't change what's happened in the past. We can only do our best to improve ourselves and help others, especially children, when we have the chance," she whispered.

He nodded sadly. With slumped shoulders, he walked to the door of the living room and turned back to Caitlin with a solemn look on his face. "I'll get the coin."

He left the room and Caitlin could hear his footsteps plodding wearily upstairs. She stood and walked to the large mantelpiece adorned with framed photographs. She recognized Seagull, looking beautiful on her wedding day to a very handsome John. Peering closer at the photo though, she noticed the smile on Seagull's face didn't come from her eyes. She felt a pang of sadness for her. Moving her gaze along to the next picture, a family one, she guessed the blonde holding a glass of wine as she leant into Spencer must be Jane. *Attractive,* she mused and jumped at the voice behind her.

"It's gone." Spencer was standing in the doorway.

"Gone? But…"

Spencer walked towards her.

"I swear to you it was by the telephone beside our bed. I'm not lying!"

"Okay, okay! Well, have you checked the floor?"

"It's not there, I tell you." Spencer sounded exasperated.

Caitlin was relieved as her cell phone went off in her bag. Grabbing it, she was reassured to see Paul's name on the screen.

"Hey, baby." She watched Spencer as she listened to Paul. Her eyes softened. "I'm okay," Caitlin nodded into the phone. "I will. See you soon." She turned slightly away from Spencer. "I love you too," she whispered and clicked off her phone.

Turning back to Spencer, Caitlin smiled brightly. "She must have it. Jane must have the coin."

Spencer was confused. "But how?"

Caitlin picked up her bag and shrugged at him. "The power of the coins, I guess. Great, huh?"

Spencer followed her out to the hallway. "Wonderful, just wonderful," he muttered as he opened the door to let her out, a resigned frown on his face.

Forty-one: Seagull

Seagull's hand, gripping her phone, was shaking. She listened nervously, not sure whether she wanted Sarah to pick up or not.

"Yes," Sarah's voice came on the phone, cold and unwelcoming.

She knew her sister had caller ID, but she still announced herself. "It's me, Seagull."

There was silence before Sarah spoke, her voice testy. "You're too late."

Seagull's heart constricted despite knowing how melodramatic her sister could be.

"What? How is mom?" she managed to ask.

"I don't see why you'd care."

"Sarah," Seagull began to cry, "I am sorry I left without telling you. I told no one. I was confused."

After another long silence, Sarah spoke in a small voice, "It isn't mom. It's dad. He's had a heart-attack. He's in the hospital."

Seagull's hand involuntarily flew to her chest, her own heart hammering as she took this news in. "Dear God!"

"More like dear doctors." Sarah's tone softened. "They expect him to recover. I miss you, Sea. I need you here. We need you here. When are you coming home?"

Seagull began to tell Sarah all that had been going on. Finally hearing herself say, "I'll be home by July Fourth at the latest." Damn Paul Somerville—that was the date on her return ticket. "Let me know if dad's condition changes. Or mom's."

"She's doing better. Back on anti-depressants. You didn't help, but she's the main reason for dad's heart attack. Too much stress."

"I'm sorry," Seagull muttered. "I didn't think anyone would miss me."

Sarah sniffled. "Sea, take care of yourself and hug Lucas for me."

Seagull smiled at the new pride she felt in her heart for her son "Hug everyone for me too. And especially yourself. I love you."

"I will. Bye."

Pocketing her phone, Seagull decided even if John had insisted Jane take care of their baby, her mother-in-law was way too over-protective. No wonder John was such a momma's boy. Seagull was about to rectify matters. Still, Seagull acknowledged, John did seem to be developing more of a spine. But she intended to make sure Lucas wasn't turned into a wimp by his ridiculously over-protective granny, and she marched out of the apartment.

The bus ride was uneventful. Seagull was beginning to feel comfortable getting around Tokyo.

She climbed the stairs to Akira's apartment, grinning at the thought of John's gentleness with Lucas. Her husband was a good man in many ways, and Seagull wondered if they could make it right with one another.

She rapped on the door and within moments, Jane slid it open. Her swollen red eyes alarmed Seagull. It was obvious she'd been crying. Sweeping past her, Seagull searched the room for her son. "Where's Lucas?" She cried, her voice raised, just as she spotted him sound asleep in a soft pile of towels. She turned her attention back to Jane who was standing by the door, staring into space. "What's wrong?" Seagull could see she was clearly upset and felt genuinely sorry for her. *Oh God, please let it not be bad news about Asa's little girl, Emiko.*

Jane began to blubber. "I have made a horrible mess of my life," she whispered.

"You?" Seagull almost laughed but instead wrapped her arms around Jane who collapsed against her as she sobbed. Seagull found herself crying too, both of them sharing and shedding tears of sorrow and grief. Seagull wasn't sure what this was about, but after a few moments, she collected her emotions and pulled away from Jane whose eyes were downcast. It must have been humiliating for this proud woman to show such weakness. Especially to her.

"Spencer," Jane spoke almost too low to hear. "I'm going to divorce him."

Seagull had never respected Spencer, but he'd always been kind to her, and she admired that he, unlike his son, her husband, worked hard and earned a good living. "Why?" Seagull asked. "What's going on? Is he upset about you coming here? He'll get over it."

Her unwanted advice seemed to go unnoticed.

"I am so lonely," Jane sighed.

"We'll be going home soon," Seagull replied softly, though she wondered if Jane was planning on staying. She wanted to ask her about Fumio who she suspected was the root cause for Jane's sudden desire to get rid of Spencer.

Jane looked her in the eye. "Don't spend your life in a loveless relationship, Seagull. If you can't patch things up with John, you'd both be better off apart."

"I don't understand. Are things that bad between you and Spencer?"

"They have been for years."

"We all have bad moments," Seagull said, wondering who had made her counselor, especially considering her recent history. "When John and I were first married, I felt desperately trapped," she confessed.

"I know," Jane said. "I knew then. I wish I'd helped more."

Seagull was tempted to pretend Jane was a fine mother-in-law who had contributed nothing but peace to her life with John, but Jane had already turned her back. Seagull fought back the biggest urge to grab her baby and get the hell out of there, after slapping Jane's face.

Seagull watched Jane as she tapped the computer keyboard and the screen came to life. "I *am* good for some things." She turned and grinned at Seagull, pointing to a webcam image of a building surrounded by cops bristling with weapons.

"Great," Seagull felt sick to her stomach. "Christ!" She could see a little blue car darting past the police cars. "Was that Asa?"

Jane shrugged. "Probably. I called and told them the location. Surprised she managed to get there so soon from downtown. I bet this city is a nightmare for getting around in a car."

Seagull felt appalled at Jane's sudden coldness. "Where is this place?"

"You going?" Jane asked.

Seagull glanced at Lucas. "I want to, but I can't. They will need someone with a cool head." She glared at Jane who laughed.

"Unlike you, I do know where to go," she said. "Me, I've got nothing to lose."

Forty-two: Akira

Akira went into the public gardens and looked all around. The smooth green lawns, the sculpted hedges next to swaths of carefully raked white pebbles, and the clear water of the lily pond reminded him of the Pure Land Gardens. A rush of sadness enveloped him as he remembered his time spent there with his master, Joumi. He longed to see him again.

What would his old friend do? he wondered as he stopped in front of the tranquil water so similar to the Ajiike pond. Dropping to his knees, he dipped a hand into the clear liquid, gazing at his own reflection. *Oh Master.* Akira sighed. *There are such troubles happening and I don't know how to help.*

He ran his fingers through the water, making a nearby lily glide gracefully across the surface. It made him think of Asa. She was as graceful as a lily too. Wouldn't it have been great if she *had* turned out to be his mother? If Emiko *had* been his sister, he could have let her know he didn't really hate her that he didn't want her dead, he wanted her alive. Akira smiled forlornly. Still, at least there was a chance to reunite this Emiko with her mother, even if *his* hope of finding *his* sister was gone.

He suddenly noticed the same lily gliding back towards his hand. He splashed the water to make it float away. It swept a few yards distant and seemed to dart back towards him, riding high across the ripples. So he did it again. "Haha!" This was fun. It was almost as if the lily were playing with him. As he splashed harder and laughed louder, he didn't notice the figure behind him until he saw the man's shadow reflected in the water.

"Akira? Is that you?"

Akira jumped up, taking in the old man in monk's clothing. "Joumi?"

"It is you! No, no, I am not Joumi. I'm sorry, Akira. You know he died. Except for the robes, I don't even look much like him. But I can understand your confusion. It's been a few years. How are you?"

Akira peered into the man's face and smiled as recognition set in. "Daichi!" He threw himself into the old man's robes, almost knocking his frail frame to the ground.

Daichi staggered back, laughing gently and hugging the boy to him.

"I've missed you, all of you, especially Joumi." The pain and tension of the last few days coupled with the sure knowledge that his master was long-dead overwhelmed Akira. He began to sob.

"Shush, child," Daichi soothed. "I miss him too. Everything will be all right."

"What are you doing in Tokyo?" Akira managed to ask through his tears.

Daichi hugged Akira tighter as he replied, "Ah, a friend. Unfinished business. Now tell me, why the tears?"

Akira sobbed harder. "I don't know what to do, Daichi!"

Daichi's knees creaked as he lowered himself to look at Akira. "What is it boy? Are you unhappy? I thought you were with your new father."

"I am. He is very sweet." Akira grinned, knowing Haruo would not like to be called *sweet*. "There are terrible things happening. Again. The ten yen coins are back. I don't understand."

Daichi frowned. "Come," he beckoned to the stone bench beside the pond, "sit and tell me what's been going on."

As they rested on the cold bench, leaning against one another, the lily spun a full circle. It reminded Akira of a dancer swirling around in a music box. He almost expected to hear the tinkling sound of a shamisen.

Once Akira had finished telling Daichi about what was happening with the girl Emiko and all the Western people who were somehow caught up in this, he waited for the old man to speak.

Daichi, however, just sat nodding his head.

Akira nodded too, imitating the old man.

After several long silent minutes, Akira could wait no longer. "Well?" He asked.

"Hmm?" Daichi looked up confused. "Well what?"

Akira rolled his eyes. "What *can* we do?"

"We?" Daichi blew a soft breath of air from his lungs. He turned his face to Akira's. "Oh no, dear boy. I'm no Joumi. He was the bodhisattva amongst us. I suggest you leave it to the police."

"But what about the coins and why did the Westerners receive them?" Akira stood up and stamped his foot petulantly.

"Sit down, child!"

The authority in the monk's voice made Akira obey. He plopped onto the bench next to the monk, muttering, "Sorry."

"So we just wait?" Akira stared across the pond. He cocked his head sideways, listening intently. He stared at Daichi. "How can you make such a promise if you don't know?" he demanded, his voice quivering.

"Huh?" Daichi stared at him.

"I said how can you promise if you don't know?" Akira repeated, worrying the old man was deaf.

"I know what you said, Akira, but why do you question *me*? I never promised anything. I never uttered a word."

"You said *there's a reason for everything and in time it will become clear. I promise.*"

"No. I said nothing."

Akira's mouth dropped open and he blinked at Daichi. He studied the water lily which floated silently on the pond surface. "Joumi?"

"Perhaps," Daichi acknowledged.

As they both watched, the lily dipped, sinking below the surface then popped up out of the water.

They turned back to each other and smiled.

Forty-three: John

John watched a monk in long crimson robes walk over to Akira who was dipping his hand into the water of the pond, splashing a water lily so it floated back and forth making wide ripples. He ought to go over, but something told him to leave them alone. The boy was safe, even without his dad Haruo to make sure. He felt gratified Haruo trusted him to take care of Akira. Also a little scared. If something happened to his son, God knew what he'd do to John.

When John had told the others it was Jane on his cell, Fumio almost snatched the phone from him, putting his head close to John's in an attempt to hear what Jane was saying. The guy had grinned from ear to ear when she said she'd hacked into the police computer. "Asa," he'd shouted gleefully, turning to his sister, before John had even hung up, "Jane's found out where the kids are being held."

Clearly, Fumio was as in love with John's mother as she was with him. John wished like hell he could put a stop to their bullshit. He'd tried to call his dad to tell him to come to Tokyo fast but hadn't been able to get through. All he got was a busy signal on the home phone, and when he'd tried his father's cell, the snooty phone voice told him to hang up and try again later. He'd left a message, but who knew if his dad would get it in time.

After Haruo had crammed himself into Asa's car and they'd torn down the street with Fumio not far behind, John began to question the wisdom of having stayed with Akira. But Asa had refused to allow Akira to go with them, saying a little boy couldn't help. At the time it seemed clear to John that Haruo wanted to be there for Asa. She certainly didn't need *him*. And she was right. The middle of a crime intervention was no place for any kid. He urged Haruo, as if he needed any encouragement, to go with her. The man's eyes said it all, including his thanks to John for keeping an eye on Akira who'd gotten frantic when he was told he couldn't go. He jumped up and down bawling they needed all of the coins, all of the coins! And he only had three of them.

John got up from his bench to check on Akira who stared at him happily. "Look, John," he hollered, pointing to a water lily. "It's Joumi!"

What was going on with Akira? One moment he was angrily yelling about those worthless coins. Now he was babbling nonsense. "What are you talking about," John called out, hurrying over.

"I am Akira's friend from the monastery where he used to live." The red-robed monk bowed to him.

John felt stupid but he bowed back. "Hi, I'm John. Also his friend."

Akira grabbed John's hand and tugged him towards the edge of the water. "See," he said. "Joumi is playing with me. Watch the water lily spin."

John was puzzled but didn't want to ruin Akira's game by telling him the pretty flower was floating out to the middle of the pond probably because he'd pushed it. He was obviously excited, and his Japanese buddy was grinning too. John raised an eyebrow towards the man, hoping for him to help settle Akira down.

"Joumi," he said in fairly good English, "was my brother monk who rescued Akira. You knew this?"

"No," John shook his head. "I don't know much about Akira except he's a good kid."

"Ahhh," the monk nodded thoughtfully. "Life is Mystery. Who would think I'd come to this park in this place at this time and meet up with an old friend? We both are hoping Joumi will help us just as he did in the past before he died."

"Excuse me. I suppose Akira filled you in about the little girl, Emiko, and the other children held by those thugs. How is a dead man going to help us rescue them?"

"Rescue of the living not always so simple," the monk said.

John was exasperated. This sounded like religious mumbo jumbo to him.

Akira tugged on his hand to get his attention.

142

The lily was now in the middle of the pond and it was spinning.

The monk clapped his hands.

There must be a rational explanation. "A carp probably has it by its root," John said, feeling bewildered. Were these two Japanese playing games with him?

"No," the monk said, gently placing his hand on John's arm. "No carp. Mystery."

"You and Joumi had the same problem," Akira chimed in. "Joumi's woman leave her baby too."

John was not about to discuss Seagull with Akira or this monk who was staring politely at the ground. "My baby has never been neglected," John said. "I was always there for him."

Akira looked momentarily sad. "Haruo have no one until I show up in his life." The boy cocked his head to one side. "What?" he said as if he heard someone speaking.

This was spooky. John was scared the boy was having some sort of breakdown.

But he was the one about to have a seizure.

Something fell from the sky and dropped on his foot. At first he thought it must be a hailstone, but there were no clouds. No one was near enough to have thrown it either. It simply dropped out of the empty air. When he looked down, he saw a ten yen piece identical to the one he'd gotten back in the States and given to Akira.

The boy pounced on it. "Now I have all four." He looked up into John's eyes. "It will be okay, John, you'll see." He bowed to the monk. "Come along," he commanded.

John compliantly followed the boy and his monk buddy who had taken his hand. They waved down a cab. "Where to, John?" Akira asked.

He gave the cabbie the address he'd gotten from Jane.

Forty-four: Emiko

Emiko sat trembling in the corner of the apartment, her dark eyes wide and fearful as she peered around at her fellow captives. Her cheek was bruised and grazed. Her tears had angered her abductor who'd smashed his fist into her face to shut her up.

"Emiko," her friend Ama whispered. "Are you okay?"

Emiko tried to smile at Amaterasu, who put her finger to her lips to quieten her friend.

"The police are outside!" her friend murmured.

Emiko's heart rattled in her little chest. She managed a slight smile this time.

Ama gave a sneaky thumbs-up but quickly looked down, lest their captors notice.

Could this really be it? Could they be saved? Emiko still couldn't smile without it hurting, but her eyes lit up with hope, realizing she might soon be free of the torment she and her friends had endured these past few years since the tsunami.

The Tsunami...

"Mummy! Mummy!"

"I'm here Emiko, hang on to me and your brother!"

"Daddy?"

"Just hold on darling, please hold on!"

As the water gushed over them, she felt a thud and watched her mummy float away.

"Akira!" She wailed in terror as her brother too slipped under the water and was gone.

144

She'd gasped as the dirty salt water had flooded her mouth and stung her eyes and she'd desperately kicked her little legs to stay afloat as debris hit her face and bodies sailed past her.

"Here child! Hold on to that tree trunk!"

Emiko couldn't see who was speaking to her as her head went under the water again. As she surfaced she could hear the voice again amid the roaring of the wave. "Here, over here, girl!"

Through sore blurry eyes, she'd finally spotted the figure clinging to a partially submerged downed tree trunk that seemed to be wedged amongst other gathered debris.

She frantically began to kick her legs and paddled in the direction of the tree.

"That's it, keep going, you're nearly here!" The encouraging voice heightened her determination. She kept swimming, gasping for breath, her body getting heavier and heavier with exhaustion.

Suddenly, just meters away from safety, another swoosh of water dragged her under and she tried to hold her breath as the great ocean threatened to fill her lungs.

But then she felt something prodding the side of her head, and she desperately grabbed at it and was pulled up above the surface. Coughing and spluttering, her head emerged and she could see that she was close to the tree trunk. A man pulled her nearer with a long branch.

"That's it, deep breaths girl. I've got you now."

Finally, she reached the trunk and the man pulled her toward him, a gentle smile on his face as he held her sobbing little body.

"It's ok; we should be ok here. Help will come."

"My mummy and daddy and--"

"Shush," he'd soothed as tears streamed down his own face. "Shush."

After the powerful wave subsided, they'd clung to each other, shivering in the dirty water for several hours before eventually help came. They'd both been taken to the nearest hospital. So many people running about, so many hurt, she'd never seen her rescuer again.

She'd lain in the hospital bed, her eyes unblinking and dry, wondering if she was the only one of her family to survive. Wondering what was to happen to her without her mummy and daddy. If they were dead, she wished she had died with them.

Once her injuries and hypothermia had been treated, she was sent to a temporary care home where she was one of many orphaned children. Though the staff there tried their best, they really couldn't cope with the sudden influx of so many parentless kids. After several nights with very little food, Emiko and Amaterasu had decided, to their cost, to run away...

As the thug keeping guard of them looked out of the window, Emiko heard him raise his voice frantically to another.

"They've surrounded the whole building. We have no choice!"

Emiko sank down, wishing she could make herself invisible. Ama managed to crawl over to her. They held each other's hands tight.

"There's only one thing to do," their guard said too softly, glancing at the children. A little boy started shivering and began to cry. "Shut up, kid! You've been nothing but trouble."

The other guy, his breathing ragged, came over to him. They whispered to one another before reaching for their guns. They turned dispassionately towards the group of terrified children.

Forty-five: John

John stared in disbelief at the police barricades and yellow tape blocking their path. He'd assumed the address Jane gave them was a house, but instead the cabby had brought them to the Port of Tokyo, only a few miles away from the park where they'd been hanging out. The image of the ten yen coin falling from the sky flashed into his mind.

As soon as the driver saw what looked like a considerable force of riot police, he slammed on the brakes, screeching to a halt. He leapt out of the driver's seat and threw open the passenger doors, yelling, "Out, out!" He snatched the fare money offered to him by the monk who was the last one to climb slowly out of the cab. The driver wasted no time. He made a hasty departure.

The warehouse, a plain metal building flanked by huge multi-colored shipping containers, faced a wide blue harbor where they could see red cranes like oriental dragons rising from a concrete wharf. No ships were moored in the expansive canal except one small motorboat not much bigger than a semi-truck. A lonely tugboat chugged through the water. Behind it, skyscrapers pierced the grey sky.

"There they are," Akira cried, and darted towards Haruo and the others who were huddled together. Everyone, except Asa who did not take her eyes away from the warehouse door, saw him coming. The monk, an elderly man, couldn't keep up with the boy, but John sprinted after him.

A cop in a dark blue uniform tried to stop Akira from crossing into the cordoned-off area, but he ducked under the yellow tape and rushed by the officer.

John skidded to a halt all too aware of guns pointed towards him. He held his arms up in the air. Another policeman grabbed Akira and dragged him over to the others. Some sharp words were exchanged. Japanese. From the gestures and frowns on the face of the policeman, it was clear no further movement towards the warehouse would be tolerated.

Haruo took his son's arm and threw Asa a worried look.

"Save them!" Asa shouted.

The monk, gasping, arrived and put a gentle hand on Asa's shoulder. She shook him off.

They stood together, not saying another word, watching as several police officers bristling with weapons crept towards the building. A door cracked open and there was a loud boom.

John saw the flash from the bullet. "Christ!" he muttered, watching police drop to the ground and take cover.

Haruo tried to cover Akira's eyes. The cries and screams from the children inside the building shattered the air, seeming to rise above what had become a racket of gunfire. Haruo growled, a sound John would never forget—an agony of rage bursting from his guts. Akira was suddenly thrust into John's care, and Haruo stormed into the fray.

"Abunaikara, yamenasai!" Asa cried and tried to go after him, but between John and the monk, they were able to keep her with them.

So fast, it happened so fast. Haruo rushed the warehouse and thrust himself inside.

With guns blasting and policemen running in every direction, it was impossible to keep track. A loud police helicopter whirred overhead. Voices shouted from a loudspeaker. Suddenly, all was eerily silent. The police inched forward.

Haruo came stumbling outside, carrying a little girl who lay limp in his arms.

Nothing, not even a god could have held Asa back. She darted forward and fell to her knees in front of Haruo whose stony glare made him look like a marble statue. She gently stroked the little girl's face. "Emiko," she said.

"She saved me," the child whispered. "I am Ama, her friend."

Haruo gently deposited the little girl into Asa's arms. Fumio declared he was a doctor and began to examine the child. It was only then John noticed the blood soaking through Haruo's shirt sleeve. Haruo, with one long groan, suddenly sank onto the gravel. A torrent of Japanese words emitted from his lips like lava spewing from an erupting mountain. He began to weep.

Fumio bear-hugged Asa's shoulder. He nodded grimly towards John and the monk whose face was creased with worry. "He said the bastards got away."

"Haruo," Akira cried, kneeling next to his dad who'd fallen face forwards. The boy tried to lift him, but Haruo was too heavy for the lad.

Fumio glided away from Asa who was still whispering to the little girl and petting her face. He crouched next to Haruo, ripping the man's bloody shirt sleeve open, trying to staunch the bleeding.

Before long, a policeman, probably a senior officer, one hand on the gun tucked into his yellow waistband and one hand raised towards them approached. He punched a number into his walkie talkie. "Kyukyusha! Ambulance!" On seeing the monk, his eyes softened, but he did not remove his hand from the gun grip. He spoke gruffly in Japanese, his meaning clear. "What the hell is going on here?"

He shushed all but Asa, and listened intently, occasionally nodding, clearly observing them all. While she talked and he listened, other police, including a young woman in black uniform with white riot helmet, visor raised, came on the scene.

Finally, in fairly good English, he gave orders. "Ambulances on way. Little girl must go hospital for examination. You," he pointed to Asa, "go with her in custody of Officer Sasaki." The policewoman knelt by Asa and the little girl, talking softly. "You," he pointed to Fumio and Haruo, "go with him also hospital. Rest of you are under arrest." He grinned at the monk. "Paddy wagon for you."

Forty-six: Jane

As she closed the door of Haruo's apartment and went outside, Jane heard Seagull call out, "Good luck. Let me know what happens."

Jane paused for a moment, wondering whether she should go to the others or not. After all, the police were there, what could she possibly offer?

Her cell phone rang and she snatched it out of her bag expecting to see John or even Fumio's number on the screen. She sighed with exasperation, noting it was an international number. "Spencer," she answered without emotion.

"Jane, we need to talk."

Jane shook her head. "Not right now, Spencer, I have to--"

He interrupted just like always. "Who is this Fumio that John has told me about, hmm?"

She gritted her teeth, furious both with John for speaking to his father about her and with Spencer for the audacity to even question her after all his infidelities. "He's my boss, Spencer, and..." she stopped, suddenly wondering just what Fumio did mean to her.

"And?" Spencer's tone was sharp.

She bristled, her anger back again. "And a very good friend, Spencer. That's all you need to know."

"All I need to know? Jane, what the hell is going on with you? You take off to the other side of the world, I hear nothing except for news of these crazy fucking coins, and John leaves me a garbled message about you and this Jap!"

She heard the hurt beneath the anger in Spencer's voice and at once felt sad and sorry for him. "Spencer, please, I can't talk right now. We *will* talk, okay? Just later."

There was silence at the end of the phone. She wondered if her husband had hung up.

Then he spoke again, his voice catching. "Jane."

She found herself wiping a tear from her eye, sure he must be crying.

"Jane," he composed himself, "I'm sorry, I'm so sorry."

She waited silently and a little hostilely for him to continue. Behind her the door opened and Seagull popped her head out, giving Jane a questioning look. Jane shook her head and pointed to the cell tucked under her chin.

Seagull nodded and quietly closed the door.

"I know I've taken you for granted, Jane."

Jane was stunned by Spencer's words. After all these years, did her husband finally realize how he'd treated her? How he'd pretty much ignored her, belittled her, and undermined her ever since their son was born and she'd become a mother? Her identity as a woman and a wife, smothered with maternal responsibility, had meant nothing to him. Absolutely nothing. "Spencer, I really have to go." She wanted to end this conversation, to tell him it was too little too late. Yet part of her, too, wanted them to talk. Finally. She'd waited her whole life, it seemed, for them to be as intimate as when they'd first been lovers.

She made a snap decision. Now was not the time. The others might or might not need her help, but she wasn't about to have a heart to heart with Spencer. He'd have to wait. Like she'd waited and waited, fretted and turned to booze. She took a deep breath, trying to find the right words to end this call and quite possibly her marriage. "It's too late, Spencer. I don't think I'll be coming home."

She clicked off her phone and bolted down the steps of the apartment to hail a taxi.

She suddenly felt a lightness in her heart even though she didn't know what she might find when she got to the others. It had to be okay. It just had to be. She gave the driver the address of the block where the children were being held.

He shook his head. "Police everywhere!" He explained in broken English. "Man shot, not get near. Police block road."

Jane's heart sank. Her momentary euphoria from having said no to Spencer disappeared. She suddenly felt sick with fear. *John! What if John had been shot? Or Fumio? Oh dear God, why did I give them that address? I should have left it to the police.*

She reached into her purse and pulled out a couple of hundred dollars in yen notes. "As near as possible, okay? And fast!"

The driver grabbed the bundle of notes, grinned at her in the rear view mirror, and sped down the street.

Forty-seven: Jane

Jane stared confused at the scene outside the warehouse where the cab halted. Police cars, ambulances, a helicopter whirring overhead, and guys in black riot gear armed with what Jane, who didn't know guns from sticks, realized were automatic weapons. "Christ!" she muttered to herself. "What the hell is going on here?" Her eyes roamed back and forth in shock.

The taxi-driver turned and stared through the connecting window, pointing to the door, clearly intending for her to get out of his cab. "Just a minute." She shook her head, her voice caustic and demanding enough to cow the driver. He glared at her but stopped gesturing towards the door.

"There they are!" she cried, suddenly seeing a stretcher being loaded onto an ambulance. She couldn't tell who was on it. Nearby, she spotted John, his face glum as he climbed into an armored police wagon, a cop behind him. Another ambulance, already loaded, sped away. Jane did not hesitate. "Follow that ambulance," she commanded, grateful to know John was not hurt but desperately worried about Fumio.

They caught up to the ambulance just as medics were taking a stretcher through automatic doors into the Tokyo Medical University emergency room. At least it was familiar territory. Fumio, as part of her orientation, had showed her through various examining rooms, even introduced her to some of the staff, not that she remembered any of them now. In any case, she had no time for small talk or niceties.

She searched her handbag, pushing to one side a pint of vodka but desperately wishing to take a swig. No time. She found her wallet and thrust another bundle of yen notes through the window at the cabbie. "Wait here," she spat, but the minute she was outside and had turned her back, she heard him driving away. "Jerk!" she yelled, looking over her shoulder, watching the cab dart out into the main street, disappearing amongst the traffic.

Jane refused to waste another moment. She plunged through the entranceway into a packed waiting room in time to see the stretcher being wheeled behind double doors, a police woman following. No one was going to stop her, including the startled nurse who was yelling at her in Japanese. Jane didn't know who was hurt, but she intended to find out and make sure they got the best of treatment. As she dashed into a tiny examining cubicle, she was confronted by the police woman who grabbed her wrist and tried to drag her away from the patient, but she ripped her arm free.

"Sweet Jesus," she swore, dropping to her knees, and looking gently at the little hands of a girl holding a sheet up to a sweet little face.

"Hello," the little girl said. "I am Ama not Emiko."

Jane was stunned. "That's all right," she said, wishing she could speak Japanese.

The police woman addressed her in good English. "Who are you? What is your business here?"

Jane, caught off-guard, feeling totally disarmed not only by the tough police lady but also by the sweetness of the child, said, "Are you hurt, sweetheart?" She took the little girl's hand. The child smiled trustingly and repeated in English. "Mommy?"

"Who are you? How do you know this child?" the police woman barked at Jane, placing her hand on Jane's shoulder.

"I'm sorry," Jane responded. "I'm Dr. Jane Hudson. This little girl must be one of the children my son John Hudson was trying to free. My friend Dr. Fumio..." Jane suddenly had a mental lapse. She couldn't remember Fumio's last name. She stared at the police woman. "I am here in Tokyo, assisting one of your doctors in his medical research."

"Aha," the policewoman said. "Your son was taken to the police station with the rest of your gang."

"Please," Jane begged. "We aren't the gang you need to catch."

The officer smiled slightly. "I know," she said. "Don't worry. We will apprehend those bullies. How dare they use little children!" Her phone rang and she answered, speaking in fast Japanese.

"You didn't get them?" Jane asked as soon as the officer pocketed her cellphone.

"No. Several of them got away with the other kids. Guy by the name of Haruo wanted to be a hero. He managed to rescue this little girl, but the thugs had a boat waiting. You know the guy? Haruo? We *will* nail the creeps. Just a matter of time."

"Haruo?" Ama said, her eyes wide.

The police woman was frowning. "You knew him before?"

Jane didn't understand the torrent of words from the little girl whose eyes gazed innocently into hers, but the policewoman took pity on her and translated.

"She said she didn't know Haruo but he rescued her. She wants him to be her daddy. And guess what, now she asks if you'll marry him. I suspect she'd take anyone who'd love her, but she wants you to be her mommy."

Jane almost burst into tears. "Tell her I can't marry him. I'm already married, but I'll make sure she's taken care of." She glanced towards the police lady who bowed slightly to her and spoke to the little girl.

Jane realized she was utterly helpless in this situation, completely out of control, and unable to fix things for this little girl the way she'd fixed everything for John.

"Ama," she said, stroking the hair out of the little girl's eyes. "You mustn't worry about a thing."

The little one's face lit up like sunlight and she began to giggle. "I like you, lady. I will tell you secret." She spoke fairly good English, putting her arms around Jane's neck and pulling her close.

Jane put her ear against the child's lips.

"Emiko get to swim in the hot baths on a big island," she whispered. "Nice people live there and they going to adopt Emiko and me together, but I'd rather you did."

Forty-eight: Haruo

Haruo winced as the pretty nurse wrapped his arm in a tourniquet.

"You okay, Chichi?" Beside him, Akira touched Haruo's shoulder, his face filled with worry.

Haruo nodded, trying to smile through his pain.

"He'll be fine." The nurse nodded at Akira and patted his head affectionately.

"The thugs?" Haruo suddenly looked at Akira who was already shaking his head.

"They got away..."

Haruo sighed, shaking his head in frustration.

"But the little girl, Ama, is safe; you saved her!" Akira grinned at Haruo who cursed inwardly then looked up in surprise as Asa entered the small holding ward.

"Hi," she said tiredly, "how are you?"

Akira moved back from the bed to allow Asa to get closer to Haruo.

Haruo shrugged. "I'll live. I'm just sorry I couldn't save all of the children, especially--"

"Shush," Asa silenced him with a gentle finger to his lips.

Akira couldn't help but notice the slight blush that rose on his father's cheeks. He smiled to himself as Asa continued, "The police are after them, I'm sure they will..." She couldn't go on, her shoulders shaking as she began to sob.

Akira almost began to cry with her.

Haruo's eyes watered. He reached out a hand to Asa who gripped it hard and sank next to him onto the bed, still crying, leaning into his good shoulder.

Akira patted her back. "I am going to find out about John and Fumio." He slipped quietly from the room.

"I'm so scared, Haruo." Asa spoke in a whisper. "I am scared not just of what will become of my daughter, but of what may have already happened to her up till now."

Haruo felt the nausea in his stomach, understanding her meaning only too well. These children had been held for a long time by the greedy men in the gang. Who knew what abuse they had endured and were still enduring? It was unthinkable. "The police will catch them, Asa. You *will* get Emiko back." Haruo squeezed Asa's hand.

She nodded sadly, sniffing.

"Hey, look at me."

Asa did as Haruo asked, and he couldn't help but marvel, even in these dreadful circumstances, at her striking beauty. "Whatever has gone before, she will heal. You are her mother; you will heal her. Ok?"

It was as if a light had suddenly been turned back on in Asa. "You're right," she said with sudden willfulness, her eyes bright. "I *am* her mother. And I'm going to get her back." She jumped off the bed.

"Asa, wait!" Haruo grabbed her arm. "Don't go after them again. Leave it to the police now. Look what happened to me!" Haruo gestured at his wounded arm.

"But don't you see?" Asa was suddenly animated. "It's the coins. At first, I think coins rubbish, but now I see. Not so. Those coins are powerful. They will guide us to the children!"

Haruo groaned, not for the first time resenting those damn coins.

"But Asa, please, you can't go!" He realized he was begging now, but he couldn't help it. "Please Asa, I couldn't bear it if anything were to happen to you." He paused when he noticed Asa regarding him in surprise. "You are special," Haruo managed to mutter, his eyes fixed on Asa's as she blinked uncertainly.

At last she smiled and leaned into him, her face just inches from his.

Haruo overcome with emotion, his heart beating wildly, mesmerized by those beautiful black eyes pulling him in as if he might drown with longing, was speechless.

"I'll be careful." Asa whispered and kissed his cheek before sweeping out of the room.

Haruo groaned, hating to be so helpless in a hospital bed. What sort of man let a gentle woman like Asa go off on her own? She must have help. And if *he* couldn't be the one to stand by her, then one of the others must. Perhaps that crazy dude, John, could help. While he pressed John's number on his cell phone, he absentmindedly stroked the tingling spot on his cheek where Asa had just kissed him.

Forty-nine: John

John picked at the meal he'd accepted from Fumio who'd handed him a tray of nourishing food. Were all doctors the same? Seagull always wanted him to eat more fish too. The grilled salmon in soy sauce with honey tasted too sweet, and the vegetables looked like they belonged on the floor of a pond. It was something called shungiku which was, Fumio explained, edible chrysanthemum. Weird food, but John certainly didn't plan on admitting he really wanted steak and eggs. "I'm calling my mother," he remarked, paying close attention to Fumio's reaction. The truth was he wanted to call Seagull. He didn't know why he hadn't already.

The doctor nodded slightly and continued spooning miso soup into his mouth. After a while, a frown creased his handsome face, and he set his spoon aside and looked squarely at John. "You were lucky the police only gave you a warning. They might have put you in prison for several nights. Your monk friend probably has connections or you'd all still be in trouble. It's a wonder you haven't been deported. No doubt he's back at his temple praying for you, as if that could help matters."

John held up one hand to stop Fumio from saying anything further. He listened to his phone ringing. When Jane picked up, he swiveled around in his chair away from Fumio. "Mom," he said. "Where are you?"

"I'm here with the little girl, Ama. I had my cabbie follow the ambulance. Where are *you*? Is everyone okay?"

"We're fine. Haruo got a bullet in the arm but is going to be okay. Asa's in visiting with him."

"How's her brother?" Jane asked.

"Who?" Why didn't she use the man's name? John couldn't understand her reserve. Did she think she could fool him? "*Fumio* is here with me and Akira." He emphasized the man's name, not looking in his direction but knowing he must be listening. He was tempted to ask his mother if she'd heard from his dad but decided it was better not to and avoided the issue. "We're here in the hospital café. How about Seagull? Are she and Lucas okay?" John's stomach heaved slightly at the thought of Seagull with the baby. He could hardly bear to think she might run off again and leave the baby all by himself.

"Don't worry. Seagull is going to be a good mom," Jane murmured. "I need to tell Ama I am coming back, but then I'll come directly to the cafeteria."

John didn't want her anywhere near Fumio, "I'm leaving soon, Mom. Why don't you come on back to Haruo's apartment. I'll meet you there."

Fumio suddenly leapt to his feet.

John stared in the direction Fumio was looking.

Asa was heading towards them, her stride purposeful.

"Asa," Fumio cried loudly and practically jumped the tables to reach his sister.

"Fumio," John heard his mother murmur. He groaned inside.

"Okay, okay, Mom. We'll wait for you." John watched as Asa began to weave her way through the café tables towards them. He clicked the *end call*.

Fumio rushed toward his sister and put his arm around her, steering her over to their table, one of only a few off by itself near a window.

"Akira," Asa said quietly as she held out her hand. "Give me the coins."

"You should have stayed with my dad," Akira said, frowning.

"Your dad will be fine." Asa sighed deeply and sank into a chair opposite John. "It's probably just a flesh wound."

John wondered why she was blushing, but there again Haruo was a rugged guy and Asa was a pretty woman. "We need to let the police handle things from now on," he said.

"No!" Asa cried. "Akira, give me the coins, please."

Akira plopped on the chair next to her and obediently dropped the four ten yen pieces into the palm of her hand. She carefully placed them one on top of another in the center of the table. "How do they work?" she asked Akira.

"I don't know." He was glum as he mumbled; "My master will help." He stared at the ceiling and closed his eyes.

Fumio rolled his eyes in disgust. "I don't see how your monk friend can help now. Didn't you say he went back to the monastery?"

Akira stamped his feet. "Not him. He friend of Joumi. Joumi is my master."

John glanced over Akira's shoulder. It figured. Here was his mother approaching. He only hoped Jane didn't decide she needed to take charge. Her smile was not for him, he discovered as she went up to Fumio and kissed him on the cheek. "I was worried about you."

Fumio got up, holding out a chair for her, his eyes alight with what John hoped was merely compassion from a younger man for an older woman. Jesus Christ, his mother was fifty, at *least* ten years older than Fumio.

"Is your dad okay?" Jane asked, a concerned look on her face as she surveyed Akira whose eyes were still closed, his face grave and pale.

The boy nodded without looking at anyone.

Jane stared at the coins. "There are four of them. I don't understand."

John shrugged. "Your coin arrived, no thanks to you." He had no intention of saying her coin fell out of the sky. She wouldn't believe him anyway, not that he gave a rat's ass what she thought, mooning over Fumio the way she was. He glared at her, but she ignored him, turning her attention to Fumio.

"I know this sounds crazy," she said, "but I want to adopt Ama. Do you think it would be possible?" She was beaming.

Asa snorted. "What, you want to take that little girl away from Japan? Hasn't she suffered enough changes? She belongs here."

Akira slammed his hand on the table, making the stack of coins tumble. "Izu Ōshima," he shouted, his eyes now wide open.

Fumio was nodding and Asa was holding her hand over her mouth. "They are there?"

"Where?" John and Jane both exclaimed.

"It's a volcanic island south of Tokyo."

"We must go." Asa leapt to her feet, but Fumio grabbed her hand to prevent her from dashing out of the canteen.

"Wait," Jane said. "Let's at least form a strategy." She looked over at John. "I knew you were worried about Seagull and Lucas, so I called her and told her to bring him over. She's on her way." She added sheepishly, "She might have some ideas."

John had a good mind to tell her to mind her own business, but the gravelly voice of Haruo interfered, and there he was like some outlandish apparition, except too real, wearing faded blue jeans with a hospital gown drooping over his shoulders, one arm in a sling, bandages crisp and fresh.

"You're not going without me," Haruo growled.

"Father!" Akira cried, leaping up and wrapping his arms around Haruo's waist.

Haruo hugged his son before gently setting him aside. With a grin on his face but a serious expression in his eyes, he bowed to Asa and Fumio then to John and Jane. In broken English he said; "Izu Ōshima very good fishing." Then breaking into unintelligible Japanese, Haruo began chattering with Akira, his voice raised in excitement.

"What?" John asked impatiently. "Will someone please translate?"

"If I'm not mistaken," Jane responded, "he said he has a big boat and we can all go with him to the island."

Haruo nodded. "My ship plenty big. Not fast. We all go."

Fifty: Akira

As the gyosen set sail, the dark clouds above threatened rain. Akira felt disconnected. It was as if he could see and hear the others but was somehow outside of them, somehow in the past, looking back. It had always been so, but something new beckoned, something he could not guess, something that made him shake with fear.

Jane shivered, pulling her jacket tighter around her.

"Ok?" Fumio was beside her, his handsome face full of concern.

Jane nodded with a small smile.

"Did you let Dad know where we were going?" John's shout from the other side of the boat startled Jane.

Her face showed her irritation. "No. Did you?" she replied curtly and turned her back on him to stare out across the ocean.

"Hey," Fumio nudged her gently with his elbow, "we didn't get much work done yet, did we?"

Jane looked up and giggled at the teasing glint in his eye.

"Well, hopefully when all this is over, we can finally get started?"

Fumio, however, was shaking his head. "You'll need to get home."

Jane gazed at him for several moments considering this, but she didn't reply.

John cursed under his breath as he watched the exchange between his mother and *that* man.

"Lighten up, John, your mother's a grown woman," Seagull calmly observed.

John bristled at her cold tone and snorted. "Ha! She's also a married woman, not that it seems to mean anything much to anyone these days, right?"

Seagull had the good grace to look ashamed. "John, I never meant to hurt you, I…"

"But you did." John glared at her, glad of her embarrassment.

Seagull raised her hands up in defeat and went to sit next to Akira.

"How're you doing, buddy?" She put her arm around his shoulders and hugged him in close, but he giggled shyly, pulling away.

Seagull, her face turning pale at the constant rocking of the boat, ruffled his hair.

Akira patted her knee. He shouted something to Haruo in Japanese and Haruo called back over his shoulder in reply.

Akira shrugged and took Seagull's hand. "My dad says there's a squall coming in. We may be at sea for two days. You be okay?"

"A squall?" Seagull's voice rose in concern. She looked paler than ever.

Akira squeezed her fingers to reassure her. He could tell she felt sick and scared. He felt very grown-up until Asa spoke in urgent Japanese to Haruo, asking if there was any way they could speed up the boat. One look at her terror reminded him of his own. They were both tsunami survivors.

Haruo shook his head at Asa. "Don't worry," he said, his voice steady and his weathered face strong, easing the panic in her distraught face. His hand tight on the wheel, he motored steadfastly through the choppy sea.

Everyone got quiet, listening to the waves slapping against the boat as the wind picked up.

"Come here, Akira." Haruo beckoned the boy over to where he stood at the stern.

Akira let go of Seagull's hand and obediently went to his father's side.

"What's up, Chichi?" Even though his voice sounded calm, Akira knew his father could tell he was afraid.

Haruo, his eyes still on the water battering against the boat, bent down to mutter in Akira's ear. "I need your help."

Akira nodded and listened. "Wakarimashita otou-san." Akira understood his father only too well. He bowed his head and went to the back of the boat, hoping the others wouldn't notice him closing his eyes and breathing deeply. He didn't care if they thought him strange, but he didn't want them to pick up on the danger heading towards them. *Master, Master?* He cried in his mind, flinching at the sound of thunder rumbling closer. He didn't know if he could remain calm. He heard Asa's gasp, but he continued to focus the best he could. *Master, we need your help. There is a storm coming. My dad says it looks like a big one...*

"Oh my God!" John shouted, breaking Akira's concentration.

Jane was now sandwiched between John, who had the baby in his arms, and Fumio whose hand firmly grasped the rail. All of them were staring at the sea.

Akira followed their gaze. A huge wave chased their small boat, rapidly gaining on them.

Asa was hunched over, shock in her eyes. "Tsunami," she screamed.

Akira trembled and almost froze, but somehow he ran to Asa and wrapped his arms around her, all the time praying and hoping his master would hear and be able to change the course of the deadly wave.

Fifty-one: Akira

Akira felt suddenly very present, very real, more than he ever had since the days when he'd almost drowned. He watched John crawl back to Seagull, clasping the baby, trying to shield them both from the impending wave racing behind their little boat. Fumio and Jane sank to their knees, facing one another. Tears streamed from Jane's eyes whilst Fumio gently held her face in his hands.

The wave was **nearly** upon them. Salt spray stung Akira's eyes, **almost** blinding him.

Haruo, at the helm, desperately tried to hold the boat steady, trying to outrace the giant wave.

"Haruo," Akira shouted, his voice more like a man's than his own. He knew it must be Joumi speaking through him. Somehow Haruo, his adopted dad, heard him over the tumult of the sea, waves crashing all around them, splashing into the boat and saturating everything. "Haruo, turn the boat towards the storm!"

Haruo did not hesitate. He wrenched the wheel hard and the boat turned almost on its side, causing nets and people to be thrown away from the wind.

Akira found himself gripping Asa's ankle. A giant swell raised the boat high above the sea **and** slapped them down as water swamped the boat. Akira was not strong enough to hold on to Asa. He watched in horror as the petite woman was swept overboard.

"Asa," he screamed, his voice shrill. "Asa!" He threw himself after her, aware he was crying *mommy, mommy* just like he had so long ago. But as he plummeted into the water and rose back to the surface, gasping for breath,

Asa was gone. A wooden pallet bashed against his chest and Akira grabbed it, his hand clenching the soft wood aware, even as he began to lose consciousness, it was disintegrating in his grasp.

~ * ~

There was a man walking on the water and Akira stared in fright. "Master?" he cried hopefully. But as the man drew closer, he could see it was not his master, Joumi, but another man he did not know. A hand grabbed his wrist. "Don't be scared," the man said, gently drawing him up onto the surface of the water as if he were weightless.

"Who are you?" Akira demanded to know, his legs trembling.

"I am Haruo," the man said.

"No, you are not!" Akira cried angrily. "You are not my father."

The man's voice was soft, and his eyes were gentle. "I am Haruo's namesake. I am his uncle, Amaya's brother."

"Where is my Master? Am I dead?"

"Come, I am going to take you to the Pure Land." He held Akira's hand and they began to walk. The sea was no longer turbulent but serene and empty. Akira suddenly let go of the man's hand and started to run and jump as if he were on a rubber trampoline.

He somersaulted and jumped high into the air, feeling joyous. Before long they had moved towards a cloud so dense they couldn't see through it. As they entered, it felt warm, wet, and somehow welcoming.

On the other side of the cloud, they found themselves in a garden overflowing with flowers, smelling of gardenias. Akira could hear the sweet notes of a shamisen being played and there was a woman sitting near a pond smiling at him. She stopped her tune and patted the ground by her feet.

"Don't worry," she said softly. "I am Amaya, your daddy's mummy. I have so wanted to tell him how much I love him, how sorry I am to have deserted him, how--"

"If I am dead, where is my mother? Where is my little sister?" Akira felt angry.

"Ah," Amaya said.

Her brother, who was standing nearby nodded to her.

167

"Your mother and sister are in another heaven. They said to tell you they miss you, but you are not to worry about them anymore. They are very happy and will always look over you to keep you safe."

Akira began to cry, loud sobs engulfing him. He felt the lady Amaya's hands tenderly stroking his back. "Where is my Master? Is he in another heaven too?"

Amaya's face beamed. "Here he is," she said.

Akira saw the face of a young man glistening above the blue pond. At first, he didn't understand. Joumi, his Master, was old and wrinkled, but this person, this apparition had smooth skin and radiant eyes. Suddenly, Akira smiled. It was his Master. He would know those kind eyes anywhere.

"You must go back now," the Master said, his lips did not move but somehow Akira heard him inside his head and heart. He did not want to leave this place of such love, but he knew he must. His work was not done.

~ * ~

Akira woke up in the stern of the boat with Haruo bending over him, wiping his face with his big hand. "**Buji de, yokatta.** Thank God, you're still alive," he said through gasps.

Fumio sat back on his haunches. "He will recover." He stared out to sea, his eyes roving back and forth, trying to find his lost sister.

Akira vomited. Water poured out of his stomach and lungs. As the spasm ended, he looked into Haruo's eyes. "She loves you, Daddy," he said.

Haruo's eyes filled with tears. "Asa is gone," he wailed.

Akira remembered Asa being swept away. "No," he said. "No! It will be all right! It will!"

"I hope you're right," he heard John mutter, and saw he had his arm around Seagull, who was leaning against him, whilst Jane held the crying baby in her arms.

"It's a miracle we survived," Jane cried, her eyes far away. "Look!"

Ahead of them, they saw a mountain rising above the sea.

"Izu-Oshima," Haruo said as he tried to start the boat's engine which wouldn't turn over. Fortunately, the tide was washing them towards the shore. "Perhaps the gods are with us."

Fifty-two: Asa

She'd grieved the loss of her family for so long. The physical pain had been a ceaseless fire in her body, refusing to be quelled, so much so Asa didn't recognize the sudden peace engulfing her at the same time as that huge wave.

Poor Akira, he'd tried so hard to save her.

She hadn't even fought to stay afloat once she'd entered the cold menacing ocean. Asa understood only too well its power. How could she not? The wild, unforgiving sea had taken her family and with it her soul.

Now she freely allowed it to finish the job and take her completely. She was tired of struggling to stay afloat. She was letting go, finally.

Smiling, Asa opened her mouth and took a deep breath. When water would fill her lungs, she knew it would be her final breath

~ * ~

You shouldn't be here.

It's not your time.

There is more to do.

Asa was confused by the voices. Who was speaking to her?

As she floated in the womb-like darkness, she opened her eyes but could see nothing except a faint shaft of light at the bottom of the ocean.

She found herself swimming towards it.

Go back Asa, do not swim to the light.

Go back. Go back...

She looked around, searching for the source of these words. There was nothing but black surrounding her. Yet below her there was a light, a beckoning light.

From the glow on the ocean floor, a dark watery figure appeared. Asa squinted, trying to make sense of the liquid form.

"Asa?"

Her heart began to race at this familiar voice. Could it be he? Her husband? She thrust herself, arm over arm, desperately struggling towards him, watching two smaller forms appear at the man's side.

Asa was sure she was crying, but her tears melted in the vastness of the ocean.

It was her lost family, still here, living in the sea that had claimed them.

She swam faster, desperate to get to them, yet all the time still hearing those strange unfamiliar voices urging her not to go.

You have to go back, Asa.

Stay away, Asa. It is not what you think.

She didn't understand, she was so desperate to reach her family, but suddenly it felt like there was an invisible force stopping her from swimming further down.

"I can't reach you!" Asa cried to her husband as she saw the despair in her dead children's eyes.

Her husband held his arm out to her, and she pushed herself hard against the invisible barrier but couldn't get to him.

"Mummy!" Her son was calling her and she thrust forward again, managing to get a little deeper and closer to them.

No, Asa, don't do it!

"Mummy!"

"Asa!" Asa's family called her towards them as the other strange voices begged her to stay away.

She needed to be with her family, she needed to see them. She needed to reunite with them.

As she prepared herself for a final thrust to reach them, Asa heard words that took hold: *Emiko still needs you. Alive!*

Her arms fell limp to her sides. She stopped kicking her legs. Emiko. Emiko needed her.

Her family was so close, so near she could almost touch them and hold them again. But she saw a sad resigned look on her husband's face.

With her eyes, she pleaded to her other two children. *Please understand.*

If she were to go to them, she would be deserting her only living child.

Asa's husband nodded and smiled sadly, wrapping his arms around their two children. They were all together. She would surely see them again but not now. It was time to let them go.

Asa's hand touched her mouth. She kissed her fingers and blew the kiss towards her dead family, wishing she could hold onto them forever. With the last remaining breath in her body, she propelled herself towards the surface of the water.

Fifty-three: Seagull

Seagull sank onto a low couch, hardly able to believe she'd been here on the island for two days. The horror of watching Akira being swept away still filled her mind. And Asa. She could hardly bear to think about watching her go under. Dear God, Haruo had dived in after them. How he'd managed to get hold of Akira, impossible to say. They had managed to drag the two of them back on board. Fumio had brought the boy back with mouth-to-mouth resuscitation. Haruo had sat nearby, looking stunned, gasping for breath. After Akira revived, he had tenderly wiped his son's face.

The wonder of their having survived had been explained away. It hadn't been a tsunami from an earthquake, like before, but a massive wave from an impending storm. Rain still poured down torrentially, leaving no doubt they'd been immersed in the onset of a typhoon. But the fact they hadn't all been lost at sea, that was surely miraculous.

An old traditional Japanese woman with a gentle smile shuffled about. She wore a kimono and as she served them tea, she cooed at Lucas, telling them not to worry, not with words but through gestures of love. Seagull trusted her completely with Lucas who seemed oblivious to the danger he'd been in. Seagull not only liked this woman, but was grateful at how this stranger had brought them all together. Fumio sat near Jane, John held the baby against his heart, and Haruo had his good arm slung around Akira's shoulder. Seagull rested her hand on John's arm.

When this petite woman had found them on the beach she had rushed them into her house They'd all been soaking wet, half drowned. She'd given them warm robes and asked no questions, lighting a charcoal fire to take off the chill.

As Seagull sat musing about what had happened, she felt overwhelmed, but it was simple really. How could she continue to practice medicine and be a mother? She wanted both. She wanted John back and she hoped it might be so. His care of her, his macho protection during the storm had warmed her and made her feel safe. He seemed to have forgiven her, but she knew they would have so much to figure out, so much to understand, so much to discuss.

For now, though, here on Oshima, there was little time. They had no idea where the kidnapped children had been taken. They could only hope to be able to help those who had lost their homes. Not a tsunami, no, but floods and high seas and mudslides that had buried houses and destroyed lives, creating havoc.

~ * ~

In the afternoon, Seagull was glad to go with Fumio to help. Gulls swooped in circles above her head, their keeling cries urging her on, making her grateful for the doctor skills she could use to assist Fumio. He was all business, having set up a temporary hospital, where many were bringing their loved ones, dug out from the rubble. Some had crushed arms, others had broken ribs, and all were in need of medical care.

Fumio assigned Jane to triage. Seagull liked her much better for her compassion and courageous evaluation of people, sending the most needy for immediate care. They didn't have any drugs, and they desperately needed pain-killers, but these were brave people. They endured having their wounds cleaned and bandaged; trying not to cry out when their broken limbs were splinted with anything strong enough to prevent further fractures. Seagull even used a wooden spoon on a child's broken wrist, gesturing to the mother to make the girl keep it on until she could be gotten to a hospital.

Seagull, at last, during a lull, went outside, walking away from the makeshift medical center. She came across Haruo desperately digging mud away from a house almost totally immersed in sludge. Clearly, with his injured arm, it was very difficult. Akira stood nearby watching, and she went over to the young boy. "You okay?"

"Yes." His big eyes sought hers. He was such a gentle lad.

"Sure?" she asked, putting her arm around the boy's shoulder and hugging him to her.

"Haruo, he hurt bad," Akira said.

Seagull's heart sunk. What could she say? How could she help? "He is a very good man," she mumbled.

"Yes. He make me his son, you know," Akira smiled sadly. "He need more than a son." He looked wisely into Seagull's eyes.

It was as if she was looking into deep dark wisdom, something beyond her and beyond any young child. She waited. "What more?" she finally whispered.

Akira seemed not to understand but then grinned at her sensually. "He needs a woman he loves!"

Seagull was shocked. "Of course," she murmured. "We all need love." She yearned, at that moment, for scalpels and bandages, not this boy's mysterious ideas about love which she feared were all too carnal. How could a child have any conception about sexuality?

"No," Akira said, shaking his head, as if he'd read her mind. "No! Not that!"

Seagull wished she could fly into the sky with her namesake gulls dipping on the wind, flying free. What was going on here with this child who seemed not a child?

But all at once he was a kid again and he ran towards Haruo yelling, "Daddy, daddy, guess what? You'll never guess."

Seagull watched Haruo looking gruffly at his son, but his eyes were tender. "What?" he said, putting his shovel aside. "I am busy."

"I know, Father, but you are digging in the wrong place. No one buried there. She not buried anywhere."

Haruo's eyes grew stormy.

Other men and women were digging and scraping away the slime to reveal the crushed remains of a house that had once been simple and beautiful. Suddenly, a woman shouted to the others in an excited voice.

Seagull understood nothing, and for a second hoped they'd found someone alive, but they were shaking their heads.

Seagull didn't hear Fumio and Jane walking up behind her, but she was grateful for Fumio's interpretation. "No one under rubble," he said.

"They probably had enough sense to get the hell out before the storm struck."

Akira grabbed Haruo's hand and dragged him over. "Daddy never listens to me," he said, almost gaily. Haruo's face was glum as Akira reached into his pocket and held out the ten yen coins. "We find them. We find all of them!"

Seagull was not pleased to see those damn coins. What could this boy think—that they were magic?

John walked towards them, his shoulders were stooped and he had a shovel in his hand. He spoke with a grim face. "I have no confirmation, but word is there are people trapped in a volcano shelter. Someone said they heard children's voices."

Fifty-four: Asa

Asa spluttered and coughed, eventually managing to expel the seawater from her lungs. Almost immediately she began to vomit. The spasms over, she wiped away bile that stung her eyes. She cupped one hand into the ocean and used the salty water to rinse her face.

"Emiko!" she screamed the word, allowing in oxygen. "Emiko," she screamed again, knowing her daughter couldn't hear her, nor she feared would the others. Haruo's boat was long gone.

How long was I under the water? She wondered as she gazed at the now calm ocean. Water, miles and endless miles of water, surrounded her. At least, she thought gratefully, there was no sign of sharks.

She frantically kicked her tired legs, treading water, knowing it a fruitless effort. She did not even know which way to swim to find land. She put her head back and lay atop the ocean, floating, glad of the emptiness all around her. She knew she had no chance of surviving. For some reason, she began to laugh, a deep, raucous, no-fuck-to-give-anymore kind of laugh.

She was going to die.

"What?!" she shouted, once again paddling to stay afloat, to the gray sky. How her legs ached.

"Fuck you!" She laughed at a beam of sunlight breaking through the clouds, shining upon her face.

"Fuck you, fuck you, fuck you…"

She couldn't help herself and began to cry. *Dear little Emiko. Who would help her daughter?*

At last she wiped tears from her face and groaned at the pointlessness of them. Yet they continued to fall even from her closed eyes.

Kibō o ushinawanaide kudasai!

Her eyes flew wide open. These words sounded inside her head, but she knew the voice was not hers.

Do not lose hope!

This inner male voice was unfamiliar to her. Could she be hallucinating? Surely, that must be it, dehydrated and deteriorating as she was.

I am Joumi. I am with you, Asa. Help is coming. Do not lose hope. Kibō o ushinawanaide kudasai.

Convinced she was in the last wild crazy throes of death hearing strange voices, her sore eyes dried out from the relentless splashing of seawater, she stopped focusing. She began to shiver, no longer able to feel her legs.

She began to whisper the words she'd heard in her head. *Do not lose hope. Kibō o ushinawanaide kudasai...*

Concentrating on her desperate chant, she didn't at first hear the humming of the engine. Her weary body couldn't stay afloat. Not a minute more. Her face sank under the surface, the salt water filling her nose and stinging her eyes. *Do not lose hope. Kibō o ushinawanaide kudasai.*

Somehow she managed to raise her head briefly above the water. She listened hard. A boat was coming. It must be Haruo coming for her. What a dear man, older than she, but strong.

Under she went again.

Kibō o ushinawanaide kudasai...

She bobbed to the surface and squinted into the distance towards the sound. It was getting louder and louder, coming closer. It must be a speed boat. She hoped it was a speed boat.

Kibō o ushinawanaide kudasai...

Hope suddenly *did* fill her body. She managed to somehow raise her aching arms, but once again she sank, knowing no one would see her if she went under. Her mouth full of ocean, she gasped, choking and coughing. "He...he...help!" Her voice was barely a whisper, but she continued to force her vocal chords to function.

"Help!" she found renewed strength and frantically waved her arms. Every time her head surfaced from the sea, she could see the boat getting closer.

Kibō o ushinawanaide kudasai...

It was coming for her. She was sure. The slender white boat knifed through the sea. She could see a blue stripe on its bow. There were words painted on its side. The boat was almost upon her. At last she could make out the name. *Japan Coast Guard.*

"Arigatou, arigatou, arigatou," she moaned. 'Thank you, thank you, thank you."

When the crew fished her out of the sea, inside she was still thanking them and that inner voice too, "Arigatou. Thank you."

She had not lost hope, and she was going to be saved.

Fifty-five: Jane

Jane and Akira, at Seagull's insistence, walked away. The salt air stung Jane's face. She was a little angry to have to go check on Lucas, angry to not be included with the medical team comprised of Seagull and Fumio. Oh! How she yearned for that man. But his words haunted her—hadn't he said right before the storm she needed to go home? Surely he didn't mean it.

"They need us," Akira said and jingled the ten yen pieces in his pocket.

"They're just coins, Akira." Jane remarked, biting her tongue, not wanting to take away Akira's childish belief in supernatural mumbo-jumbo. Although she had to admit she'd thought their escape from the storm did seem miraculous. Yet even that could probably be explained rationally. "Just coins," she reaffirmed.

"My master, Joumi, entrusted them to us," Akira said. "You and I. We need to go with others to rescue the children."

"Right now we are going to check on baby Lucas. Maybe that's what your…err…master meant." Jane felt helpless and irritated to be consigned to childcare as if she had no brain or skills. "They don't need us," she said softly. "They've got more than enough people to dig out any survivors."

Akira grunted a low guttural noise, sounding a lot like his adoptive dad, Haruo. "Maybe we need them," he muttered.

Jane slung her arm around the boy's shoulder, remembering John as a lad. He'd been highly imaginative too. She'd tried to streamline him into a scientific career. Spencer was the one to encourage their son's creative abilities. The funny thing was, in spite of John not earning any money as a writer, she felt proud of him for sticking to his guns and doing what he wanted. "I should have done the same," she said out loud.

"Joumi says it is not too late." Akira glanced at her and gave her a lop-sided grin, before running ahead and dashing into the house of their kind hostess.

Jane followed, bowing to the lady, aware of how orderly her house was. The Japanese woman, dressed in a bright yellow kimono with a deep pink sash around her tiny waist, held her finger to her lips and led Jane to the baby in a nearby room.

Lucas was sleeping peacefully. Two pillows on either side of his precious little body prevented him from rolling off the straw mat onto the polished wooden floor.

Jane settled onto a chair and looked at a photo on a nearby table of a much younger Japanese woman, clearly their hostess, holding the hands of two small children. They all had big smiles on their faces. For some reason Jane was reminded of her shortcomings as a mother. She'd taken care of John, yes, but this woman clearly reveled in her maternal role. She obviously played with her kids. She was a mom in capital letters: M. O. M.

Jane felt woefully inadequate. Damn, but she needed a drink. Yet she was glad no liquor was forthcoming. She wanted a clear head. Bone-tired, her head fell forward in a doze.

Laughter from next door awoke her. Akira and the lady were giggling together, probably enjoying a game. Damn, she needn't reproach herself about John. She'd done her best as a mom. She kept her eyes closed but their chuckles eventually got the better of her. After glancing at Lucas who was still sound asleep, his little chest going up and down rhythmically, something felt odd. Her eyes searched the room.

In the doorway, a shadowy young woman stood watching her.

"Asa," she gasped. The fine hairs on her forearms stood on end.

The apparition said nothing.

Jane stared back. What was this? A name formed in her mind. *Amaya*.

The figure began to fade from view, but before it disappeared completely, Jane felt herself immersed in love. It warmed her through and through.

Amaya, Jane knew, was Haruo's mother; the woman who'd abandoned her child so long ago and was long dead.

What could it mean?

Jane didn't want to believe in the supernatural. She was a scientist for Christ's sake. This could not have happened. But it had. And that feeling of love was still enveloping her. It's what everyone wanted and needed, she realized. It was what she'd always needed so badly, love.

How often she'd been mean to Seagull, recently justified by the silly girl running away from her baby. *I didn't run away. I did my best as a mom. I set a good example as best I knew how.* Seagull's mom though, Jane suddenly understood, was not a good example. She wasn't strong. Her depression and suicide attempts had surely hurt everyone. This fresh insight softened Jane towards Seagull. In an instant, she also understood how jealous she'd been of her daughter-in-law—a doctor, no less, with the chance of raising her child *and* keeping her professional life. *How dare she run away!*

A little voice in Jane's head said, *but don't you run away? Maybe not through suicide attempts but through booze?*

The love Jane was still feeling seemed to free her to recognize she need not condemn herself or anyone else. Certainly her booze addiction required professional assistance—maybe she'd join Alcoholics Anonymous. Maybe they had such meetings here in Japan. Maybe staying here was her way of escaping from her problems back at home. Maybe, maybe, maybe! She wanted to start again—be young with a brilliant career ahead, but that was not possible.

Surely, there was something new for her to do? For a fleeting moment she thought maybe she would try to help Seagull who clearly needed more understanding. Jane felt her old irritation at her daughter-in-law rise. The warm love enveloping her seemed to diminish.

It occurred to her there was one thing she could do. She took out her cellphone and found Seagull's mother's number. If there was cell-phone service here, she planned to let the woman know her daughter and her grandson were okay. She punched in the number and hit send. As she heard the phone ringing, she thought maybe she'd call Spencer too. Maybe.

Fifty-six: Seagull

Fumio grabbed up his cell phone as soon as it began to ring. Seagull stopped what she was doing to watch him take the call. "Asa?" he bellowed. "Asa, is that really you?" His eyes, full of joy, met Seagull's. "Where are you, Asa? Are you okay?" Fumio gave Seagull a thumbs-up sign. "Asa is alive and well!"

As she heard him repeat his sister's name, the smile that lit his handsome face flooded Seagull's body with relief. She gasped in delight and hurried into the house to inform the others Asa was ok.

Finding Akira giggling with their Japanese hostess, she stopped for a second to observe them and was reminded again of how Akira must miss his mother and crave maternal affection. Haruo was such a wonderful father to him, but nothing could take the place of a mother's love. Seagull's heart sank as she thought about how she'd abandoned her own child, albeit briefly.

Akira could wait. He didn't need her right now. And she needed Lucas, suddenly desperate to hold her baby boy. She was about to open the closed door of the little bedroom but stopped upon hearing Jane talking to someone.

"Yes, I understand that, Sarah…"

Seagull's hand flew to her throat. Why was Jane talking to Sarah? What had happened now?

She was about to thrust the door open but paused to listen to Jane speaking again. She pushed the door slightly ajar.

"Well, I think you're being a little harsh on Seagull. She's had her issues but she's dealing with them. You should see her with little Lucas now, she's a natural, she's…"

Seagull raised her eyebrows. *Good Lord, was Jane actually defending her? And a compliment too? Wonders would never cease.* She quietly pulled the door closed again, continuing to eavesdrop.

"Sarah, let me finish please," Jane was saying. Her tone was firm, a necessity when talking to Sarah.

"Seagull is well aware what happened to your mom, but when she heard she was stable, there really was no reason to rush back. Things are pretty complicated here. Yes, I'm glad to hear your dad is back home and doing well too. I'll tell Seagull. Of course she'll be glad."

Seagull heard Jane sigh and smiled wryly to herself. Her sister was not an easy person to placate, and in spite of them having talked, she was sure she must be spitting marbles at her behavior of late. For sure, Sarah must be pissed to hear from Jane rather than her. It wouldn't make any difference that she'd been busy trying to patch up injured people.

"Yes, of course I will. Please pass on my regards to your parents, Sarah."

Seagull heard Jane click off her phone and another weary sigh followed.

"You can come in now, Seagull."

Seagull blushed at Jane having caught her listening in on her conversation. Sheepishly, she opened the door and popped her head around it. "How did you know I was there?"

Jane smiled tiredly and stretched her arms above her head, stifling a yawn. She nodded at the window. "I saw you coming up the path. What's going on?"

"Asa is okay." Seagull smiled, remembering the good news she'd come to impart. "Fumio is on the phone to her now. It seems the **Coast Guard Rescue** got to her in time."

"Oh thank goodness!" Jane closed her eyes and clasped her hands together.

Seagull remained standing in the doorway until Jane eventually opened her eyes and looked at her. "I take it you know who I was just talking to?"

Seagull nodded, feeling uncomfortable she hadn't been the one to call back home to check on her mother.

Jane seemed to recognize her shame and beckoned her over. "Sit 'down, Sea," she muttered softly, patting the bed in front her.

Seagull obediently sat down and glanced up at her mother-in-law who'd remained standing.

"Firstly," Jane took Seagull's hands in her own, "your mom is fine. She's receiving excellent care, and they expect her to be home any day. I had intended to speak with *her,* but it seems your sister has, err, taken control of all communications."

Seagull smiled slightly, lowering her eyelids, well aware of how controlling her sister could be. When she looked up, Jane's eyes twinkled back at her.

"Secondly, I'd like to apologize to you, Seagull."

Seagull was momentarily stunned and a little embarrassed at this sudden moment with Jane. "I, erm, there's no need, I…"

Seagull was lost for words as Jane continued. "There is every need. I mean, don't get me wrong, some of your behavior has been despicable."

Seagull almost laughed. *Here's the old Jane back!*

"But I have been a little harsh on you, Seagull." Jane waited, letting Seagull take in her words.

Seagull couldn't think of a thing to say, completely unprepared for her mother-in-law's apparent kindness.

After a while, Jane sat beside her on the bed, awkwardly putting her arm around Seagull's shoulders and pulling closer towards her.

Seagull managed to not squirm.

"Maybe we need to be working together, helping each other rather than against each other?"

Seagull had never been this close to her mother-in-law, and the embrace felt a little stiff to say the least. But when she looked into the eyes of the woman she'd pretty much despised since they'd met, she saw sincerity and, just maybe, understanding. This smart attractive woman had suffered with her own issues for so long. Maybe they weren't so different after all. She managed to smile at Jane and nodded. "I think you're right," she mumbled, suddenly grateful. "We do need to work together." She felt tears welling up and prayed she wasn't about to cry.

Little Lucas saved her. He began to bawl hungrily. Jane and Seagull exchanged what Seagull hated to admit must be a maternal look. And what's more it felt agreeable.

"I'll leave you to deal with your son." Jane got up as Seagull cooed to her baby boy. "In fact, I'm going to go and deal with my own son, I think."

"Good luck with that," Seagull called softly over her shoulder and smiled at Jane's slightly wicked grin as she left the room.

Fifty-seven: Jane

Jane walked outside, a peaceful feeling spreading through her bones after the conversation with Seagull.

She breathed in the humid air and looked up at the cloudless sky. *Oh, to be a bird. To fly freely.*

In the distance she could see Fumio talking with John and she studied them for a while, hoping John wasn't being rude to Fumio. What *was* his problem, reporting back to Spencer as if she were having some sort of sordid affair? *Ha! If only!*

Jane sighed at the thought of her husband back in America waiting for her to return. She knew she needed to speak to him, to let him know the decision she'd made. Well, she hoped so anyway. It would depend on her employers allowing her to extend her contract here in Japan.

But yes, she had decided to stay here, to make a new life for herself. The thought made her feel simultaneously liberated and sad. Sad for the marriage she had once valued though never really wanted. Sad at hurting Spencer, John too, yet liberated at the changes that were on the horizon for her.

For me! Jane's heart skipped a beat. Finally, she was doing something for herself, and she didn't feel selfish or guilty about it. But there was something else she needed to do for herself first.

She reached into the pocket of her jeans, pulled out the little scrap of paper she had torn from a magazine she'd found in the Japanese lady's house, unfolded it and straightened out the creases.

A hopeful smile grew on her face as she once again read the advertisement for *The English Speaking Alcoholics Anonymous in Tokyo*. She could do this. She *would* do this. Jane slipped the piece of paper back into her pocket and dialed her cell phone.

She needed to let Spencer know first.

He picked up on the second ring, and Jane visualized him sitting by the phone waiting to pounce on her call. *Unlikely.* She smiled wryly.

"Jane! How are you? What's going on over there?"

Jane calmly filled Spencer in on all the crazy things that had happened since they'd last spoken.

Once she'd finished, the expected awkward silence was there. The unanswered question hung threateningly between them. Jane gulped as she began the conversation that would end her marriage.

"It's him, isn't it? The Jap guy!"

Jane sighed. She'd been expecting this, and she could at least answer that honestly now. "Spencer, this has absolutely nothing to do with Fumio. This is about me."

Spencer snorted down the phone but Jane continued, "I'm going to get help with my drinking."

"I think you're probably drunk now, you silly woman! Full of fanciful ideas of a career in Japan and a young lover to boot! Ha! Do you not realize how old you are, Jane? Now stop being so ridiculous and come home now!"

Jane remained silent as she absorbed his hurtful words then she spoke again, her voice firm and controlled, belying her racing heart. "Spencer, I know you're hurting, and I'm sorry. That isn't my intention. I really am going to do this. Our marriage has been dead for a long time and you know it."

Spencer was quiet now.

"You've been unfaithful to me for the majority of our marriage and I don't blame you. I'm a mess. Correction, I *was* a mess, but I'm going to get help and get a life. Without you."

"Jane." Spencer sighed, and Jane could hear the resignation in his voice. She wished she was with him rather than having this conversation over the telephone.

"I'm truly sorry," Jane whispered and was surprised at his parting words.

"No, *I'm* sorry." Spencer ended the call.

Jane narrowed her eyes, looking at her phone. Just as she was about to redial his number, she heard the shouting in the distance and looked up.

John was running towards her.

"There's been a landslide!" he yelled. "They think the children are trapped under it!"

Fifty-eight: Seagull

Seagull, crammed next to John who was in the middle of the back seat, wished this car would go faster. His mother, Jane, was on the other side of him, behind Fumio who had commandeered the car and its driver to take them to the mudslide. "Step on it!" she cried, wishing it were a race car and not this a small red hatchback, a Honda Fit.

The driver shrugged and Fumio kept silent. The engine strained and sputtered along. They hadn't been on the road for more than a minute when Jane spoke up. "How do you know the children are there?" she asked.

Fumio took a deep breath and exhaled noisily. "This is a very small island," he said, and he translated in Japanese to the driver, before continuing in English. "Everyone knows everyone else and although there are many tourists, two seedy looking men with a bunch of scared little kids stood out. They are in a rental house near Oshima Town. It might not be them, but it most likely is. We'll know when we get there."

Seagull didn't know whether she wanted it to be them or not. Of course, she did want to find them, but not under a mountain of mud. The wide highway, empty of cars, went over a bridge across a deep ravine. They heard a loud gushing noise.

"Yare yare! Oh boy!" the driver said as he slammed on the brakes and came to a stop. They sat huddled together, stunned to watch pine trees that looked like twigs being washed off the mountain in a giant roar of water, gushing into a stream below the bridge.

Seagull's heart sank. If the kids were caught in anything like this, they wouldn't stand a chance. "Please," she said. "Let's hurry." She glanced over at Jane who looked pale.

"It's too late," Jane muttered. "Too damn late."

"You don't know that," John responded and took his mother's hand, but she jerked away.

Sounding distant and clinical, she turned and looked first at Seagull, then into John's eyes. "John," she said quietly, "I truly hope the little children are alive, but right now I am wondering if *we* will make it out of this disaster. There is something I must tell you."

Seagull felt herself cringe, pretty sure what Jane was likely to say, and she was right.

"I just told your father I am divorcing him. It's too late for us to try to repair the mess we've made of our marriage."

"You're not thinking straight." John sounded exasperated. "We *will* get out of this and once you're home, you'll change your mind."

"I'm not going back to the States for a while." Jane put her hand on Fumio's shoulder. "With your help, Fumio, I'd like to be able to stay and renew my contract."

Fumio grunted. "This is not the time to worry about such matters."

"I know." Jane stared out the window. "I'm so sorry. We have more important problems now. Have you heard any more from Asa? How is she?"

"She is on her way in the ferry. The coastguard took her to Tokyo Hospital, but she refused to stay. Akira and Haruo are waiting for her at the docks. There is no more time to waste." He tapped the driver on the shoulder and pointed to the other side of the bridge. "Isogu! Hurry!" he commanded.

The driver nodded and proceeded slowly towards the mud slide. Fortunately, although a few tree limbs were scattered across the road, the mud had swept beneath the bridge and they were able to pass without much trouble, crushing twigs and branches beneath the tires.

When they saw the remains of a small house, its white siding and partial roof protruding from beneath a pile of trees and rocks, Fumio bashed the dashboard with his fist. Many people in official blue uniforms were trying to clear the debris.

"Christ!" Jane groaned. "Thank God you didn't bring Akira along. A young boy shouldn't see this."

Seagull wasn't so sure. "We need Akira. He has the coins," she said.

"Coins will do us no good." Fumio leaped from the car and began rattling Japanese to one of the officials. After a brief conversation, a grim look on his face, he turned to them, now all standing nearby, staring at the wreck of a house. "They found the bodies of two men. Apparently, they were trying to escape but got caught in the mud. One of them was crushed under a giant boulder."

Seagull looked at Fumio's serious face. His sister's child, Emiko, might well be in the chaos in front of them. She wanted to find a way to comfort him. But what could she say? All they could do was wait and hope the children, if indeed it was them, were somehow in a safe place, perhaps in a pocket of air. It had been known for people to survive such disasters for long times.

For an hour they leaned against the car. The air was humid but no more rain came down which might have created more of a landslide. John busied himself, helping remove logs and boulders, while other workers dug out mud, slinging it into trash bins to be carted away and dumped elsewhere. When they heard the cry of a child, they stared at one another, their mouths dropping open.

"Dear God." Seagull stared fixedly on a doorway, lying awkwardly on its side, not partially cleared of the thick goo. "Please," Seagull implored. "Please!"

A man yelled into the ruined house. Then another guy with an axe came and began to whack at the door. Seagull wanted to stop him, terrified the children would be too close to the door and his axe. At last, two guys ripped away the door only to find more mud had somehow oozed into what must have once been a front room.

But there was another cry from a child somewhere further in the house.

It was such a small house, but it took what seemed like an eternity of frantic digging before a little hand was seen beneath what looked like a platform bed. The heavy wooden structure had been tossed at an angle which must have been why the kids had managed to get underneath. Two brawny men heaved the bed up and one by one, three little children crawled out.

"Emiko!" Fumio cried, rushing forward, and with Seagull's help, checked each little child for broken bones and bruises. At last, satisfied they were okay, Fumio spoke vacantly, his voice like gravel, "Where is Emiko?

None of these resemble Emiko?"

Seagull couldn't stop the tear creeping out of the corner of her eye. She saw Jane crying too. "Are there any other children?" she asked an official. "Are they still digging?"

The man shrugged, not understanding.

At last, another of the workers emerged carrying a limp child wearing blood-stained clothing out into the open, her long hair draped across her face.

"Emiko!" Fumio stared at the ashen-faced child. "It's Emiko! I know it is." He began speaking comfort in Japanese. "Hold on. We will help you."

The little girl opened her eyes briefly and almost smiled. "I knew you'd come," she whispered. "I want my mommy."

Seagull thought her heart would break. She so thanked her lucky stars that her child, Lucas, would not have to cry out, *I want my mommy*. She would always be there for him no matter what happened between her and John. She quickly set to work to examine Emiko, but what she saw made her want to drag Fumio away.

Too late, he saw the splinter like a knife, piercing the little girl's chest. "No!" he cried.

"Mommy coming?" Emiko whispered, her voice like a feather.

"Yes. She'll be here soon." Seagull spoke gently, knowing it would not be soon enough.

Fifty-nine: Asa

Asa looked coldly at the scene around her: As soon as Akira had told her the others were at a house where the children would be found, she'd gotten a taxi. Ambulance crews tended to the bodies of people they had recovered from the rubble and mud, while firefighters still searched through more debris.

"Asa! Asa!"

Asa, hearing Fumio's cries, looked up and ran towards him. "Where is she?" she screamed. "Is she here?" As she neared Fumio, the sight of his glum face stopped her. "No! Emiko, where is my Emiko?" Fumio tried to embrace her, but she saw her daughter on a makeshift gurney behind him with Seagull crouched next to her, whispering softly.

Seagull looked up at Asa with tears in her eyes as she stroked Emiko's face. She scrambled out of the way to allow Asa to kneel beside the child.

"Emiko?" Asa, unable to believe her little girl was really in front of her, kissed Emiko's head gently. A tear splashed onto her cheek. "Oh, Emiko."

"Mummy." Emiko smiled weakly and her eyelids fluttered open.

"Oh darling, my beautiful little girl." Asa touched the child's hair and pressed her face into her neck, breathing in her daughter's scent.

"Mummy." Emiko's breathing was becoming more and more shallow.

Asa flashed a desperate look at Fumio who shook his head before gulping back a sob and staring at the ground. Jane stood nearby and put her hand on his back. It was just as well. Asa certainly couldn't care for him at this moment. She turned back to her daughter, and that was when she noticed the blood.

A crimson stain seeped through the bundled up towel placed on her chest.

Emiko moaned.

Asa cried out. "No, no, no! Emiko, my sweet, mummy is here, my darling. You have to be strong!"

Asa in her fear and desperation almost wanted to shake the child, but instead she cradled her beautiful head in her arms and smothered her little face with kisses. And wept. Asa was a physician. She knew what she did not want to know.

"My mummy," Emiko murmured, and Asa felt her daughter's hand in her hair, clutching it the way she had as a baby.

Asa closed her eyes, allowing the memories to wash over her as she listened to her little girl's breathing.

How was it physically possible for a heart to break twice? How cruel was life that it would take her little daughter away from her not once but twice?

The little hand in her hair suddenly felt heavy then was gone. Asa opened her eyes and looked at Emiko. Her skinny arms rested by her side and her eyes were closed. She wasn't breathing anymore.

"Waaah!" Asa, as she looked at the lifeless body of her daughter, wailed like a wild animal. "Wake up, Emiko! Wake up!" She began gently shaking Emiko. "No! No!" She stared up at Haruo, whose hand absently stroked her hair. At her frantic expression, he pulled Akira in close to him. She understood him wanting to hold his son close, but Akira pulled away with a determined shrug of his shoulders.

When her brother fell to his knees next to her, she choked back the tirade she'd wanted to launch against Akira for seeming so cold and unfeeling. He was only a little boy. It wasn't his fault he seemed so detached. But seeing her brother's morose face, his lips trembling, she could not control her overwhelming grief, and began to scream and sob. Fumio wrapped his arms around her waist, holding onto her tightly while she screamed and sobbed over her dead child. He too began to weep, his moans mixed with her howls of grief. They'd always been close. She knew what he was thinking. He must be convinced *this* time she really wouldn't be able to survive the heartbreak.

As the medics rushed around them, Asa pushed her brother away and covered Emiko's body with her own and refused to let go. "No, you cannot take her from me again!" Fumio tried to pull her gently away from the child, but Asa possessed the strength of a mother-lion, desperate to protect her young. She clung to Emiko's little body.

"Asa, please? She is gone."

"Leave her alone," Haruo muttered. "Can't you see she needs time?"

Fumio launched into a barrage of angry words at Haruo.

Asa heard their futile arguing. She understood that Fumio's fear for her coupled with his grief had turned into anger, but after the squabble ended, when she looked at these two men who cared for her, it didn't matter. Her eyes went flat, almost as if a light had been turned out. She struggled to breathe, her nostrils flaring. Somehow through her hysteria her voice became calm. "My little girl," she whispered.

Haruo, stroking her back, spoke gently, "I am so sorry, Asa."

"I shouldn't have come back," she whispered. "I too am dead."

Sixty: Seagull

Seagull sat with her shoulder against John's in the second row of chairs in the small room within the crematorium. They'd been apprised of the procedure.

Emiko lay in a beautiful white coffin with a half-open door showing off her beautiful little girl face. The mortician had dressed her in a white kimono. In repose, she looked radiant. Behind the coffin, which was pointed towards the western realm of the Amida Buddha, was a golden archway surrounded by fragrant white and pink lotus blossoms. It was incredibly beautiful and incredibly sad.

Asa sat in front of her daughter, not crying, not speaking, numb with grief as she awaited the moment when the coffin would be closed and her daughter's body taken to the furnace. In her hand, she held white chopsticks to be used for picking out the bones from the ashes.

It was so unfair. So fucking unfair! Seagull wanted to scream. She'd so wanted a daughter, daughters, but now she was happy with her little son. He lay quietly in John's arms, fortunately not fussing. Such a good little guy. She would never leave him again. She and John had agreed to see a counselor when they got back home, and Seagull had high hopes they could work things out. John was probably going to move in with his father, Spencer, for a time, seeing as Jane seemed adamant about staying in Japan. Although, Seagull was surprised to have learned, not because of Fumio—so she said.

Fumio sat solemnly next to his sister, gazing at the coffin that held the dead niece he'd never had much of a chance to know. Seagull wondered if he was also upset about the discussion she'd overheard him have with Jane earlier. After their exchange, he'd marched into the chapel and sat next to

Asa, draping his arm around her, without a glance in Jane's direction.

These Japanese walls were paper-thin and they'd heard every word.

~ * ~

"Jane, of course I will help you stay. I want you to work with me. But you know I want more."

John, who'd also been listening, had bristled and Seagull had patted his arm.

Jane's reply to Fumio seemed to calm him though. "Fumio," they'd heard her say. "I am years too old for you. We are friends. That is all we can be. At least for the time being. I have to live by myself. Please try to understand."

They'd heard Fumio grunt. He soon came into the chapel followed by Jane who looked flustered.

"Mom," John had said a little too loudly, "Mom, just what do you think you're doing? What about Dad?"

"What about him?" Jane had replied defiantly. "I've already given him the best years of my life. I'm not living for him any more, always waiting for him to get home, his dinner getting cold. Screw him!"

Seagull had glared at both of them. "Shut up," she had hissed. "Show some respect."

~ * ~

Now they sat in silence and watched as people began to fill the chapel.

Haruo came in holding Akira's hand. Seagull knew he must want to sit with Asa, but after the row he had with Fumio at the mudslide, he clearly intended to protect his little boy from any of Fumio's fury. It was bad enough the guy had yelled at Haruo, who was a grown man able to protect himself, but his behavior towards Akira had been unjustifiable.

Seagull wished she could rid herself of the anger she was feeling. But remembering little Akira rushing up to Asa and trying to give her the coins dismayed her horribly. There was something weirdly special about them. Yet

Fumio had shoved the boy away, yelling at him that magic would not bring back the dear little girl. It was a miracle Haruo hadn't decked him but managed to keep his cool and gently led Akira away.

Now the two, father and son, sat in the back.

Other people came in quietly, gradually filling the chamber.

At last a Buddhist monk walked to the front of the room and began to chant a sutra. Fumio stepped up to an urn and added incense three times. People in the room came forward and did the same. The air filled with a pungent earthy scent. At last a red curtain began to close around the coffin. Seagull's eyes filled with tears. She could hear Fumio sobbing. Jane too was weeping. Asa, though, sat there woodenly. She had not performed the incense ritual but simply sat staring at the coffin, her shoulders rigid, her hands in her lap.

As people began to file out, Akira suddenly ran forward. *Dear God, what on earth was the boy doing?* Seagull went after him. And so of course did Haruo.

Akira fell on his knees in front of Fumio and held his hands together in front of his heart in a prayerful gesture. "Fumio," he begged. "Take these." He retrieved the four coins from his pocket and held them out to Fumio.

Fumio's eyes filled with rage.

Haruo looked about to step in front of Akira to protect him. His eyes darkened as if he might explode with rage if Fumio said one word to Akira.

Before any of them had a chance to do or say anything, Jane stood up. "Fumio," she said, "just listen to the boy. Take the coins. I know you are a scientist, and so am I, but maybe there is more to life than facts and figures." She made her way forward, and Fumio glared at her, but she held his gaze. His eyes shifted to Emiko's coffin and then back to Jane. She looked a little pale as she cleared her throat, turning to face Haruo. "I know this will sound crazy, Haruo, but your mother Amaya came to me. She was an apparition, a spirit. Her presence filled me with such love that she somehow gave me fresh understanding. And strength. She wanted you to know how much she loved you."

Haruo's shoulders twitched and his eyes filled with sorrow. Asa, who sat listening to this exchange, smiled sadly at him through lowered eyelids.

Seagull silently thanked God he'd remained calm.

"Fumio," Haruo said gruffly. "Please do as Akira asks. Accept the money."

"Yes," Asa whispered, her eyes glittering with tears. "Please. Please." She got up and stood in front of her brother beside the little coffin. "Please, Fumio," she pleaded, taking his wrist so his palm was open in front of Akira. Fumio hesitated but he took the coins with an irritated shake of his head. "Now," Asa said, her voice strangely calm. "Give them to Emiko. They will bless her." She let go of his wrist.

Fumio gently placed two coins on Emiko's eyelids. He laid another one on top of the bandage bulging beneath her kimono over her heart, and the final one he put in her hand.

Asa dropped the chopsticks and reached in and wrapped her hand around her daughter's cold flesh. "You see," she said, "she has money now and will be able to buy sweets in heaven."

"Namu Amida Butsu," the monk intoned. "Praise to Amida Buddha," he said again in English.

Asa repeated the chant, "Namu Amida Butsu," then she moaned, "My little girl! My special little girl."

Seagull went behind Asa and stroked her back. Jane stood awkwardly nearby as John came quietly forward and put his arm around her shoulder.

Haruo held onto Akira who stared up at the altar which seemed to be emitting radiant light. He began to smile knowingly. The beams, like four rays of sunshine, lit up the coin over Emiko's heart. Asa, startled, let go of her daughter's hand. "What is happening?" she cried.

Fumio, his eyes wide with astonishment said, "I don't know." He looked helplessly at the presiding monk who could only look on in astonishment.

It was very slight at first, a delicate fluttering of her eyelids, the tiniest flare from her nostrils as she breathed in air. Then, Emiko's hands slowly moved up to her face where she plucked away the coins over her eyelids.

Her eyes opened. "Mummy," she said and sat up.

As those around her gasped, Asa began to shake. "Baby girl, my baby girl." She took her child in her arms, holding her, feeling her. Wanting to make sure she was real. That she truly was alive.

Beside her, Akira grinned and Emiko suddenly spotted him over her mother's shoulder. "Boy!" Emiko sang out, her voice a little hoarse. "Will you let me play with you today?"

Akira took her hands in his. "I will. I will. Now climb out of this box and I'll fetch you some onigiri."

Emiko made a face. "No riceballs. Yuck." She snuggled her face into Asa's neck then glanced up with a little smile. "Sweets, please."

Epilogue

Caitlin fired up her laptop and sipped her coffee, enjoying the sunlight streaming into her study through the French doors that led to the pretty garden. She could see bright red roses blooming, their petals occasionally scattering on the grass in a gentle breeze.

She smiled as she heard Paul crooning along to the radio in the kitchen as he prepared breakfast. It smelled of bacon and eggs, and bagels with strawberry jam. She smiled. He made the best scrambled eggs, and she'd come to love the crispy bacon he'd learned, from her, to drain on paper towels.

She logged into her e-mails. First, she read an e-mail from Tommy. He was now her stepson, a child she adored.

Hey Dad and Cait!

How's things? I'm looking forward to visiting you again soon. Mum said she's thinking about coming too, if Richard can get some time off. Won't that be great?

JJ and Bridget have promised to buy me some new trainers when I come too! :)

I got a merit certificate in school the other day for drama, guess I take after you hey dad?

Oh and guess what? Alice has started walking! She's so funny the way she waddles about, ha ha.

Anyway, gotta run, I'm playing football with some friends.

Laters!

T x

Caitlin smiled softly as she closed Tommy's email, figuring Paul would want to reply to his son. She just bet little Alice was such a joy.

The next e-mail was from Seagull. Caitlin frowned as she saw the subject title: URGENT!!

She clicked on the message and peered into the laptop screen reading the words, shocked and happy, unbelieving and joyous. "Oh my God! Paul, get in here would you!"

Paul's face was full of concern as he raced into the study.

"What is it?"

Caitlin's mouth was still open in surprise as she pointed to the screen and allowed Paul to read Seagull's e-mail.

Paul began to smile as he read, shaking his head. "Well goddamn," he looked at Caitlin.

Another e-mail popped up. From Seagull to Paul.

Caitlin clicked on it and moved aside to let Paul read it. He began to laugh. "That bitch! She says I got it all wrong, and she's not coming back on the Fourth of July. Damn!" He laughed some more. "She burned my ticket."

Caitlin looked at him in surprise.

"There's more," Paul said. "She's heading home to Pittsburgh on the fifth. Do you believe her?"

Caitlin grinned. "I wish she would have come here first for a visit."

"You can go see her, baby."

Another e-mail from Seagull popped up. This one to Caitlin. "By the way," she read it to Paul, "tell your husband he was right about one thing. Surprisingly."

"Yeah," Paul nodded his head. "Does she say what?"

"She says you were right about what matters most; our friends, our families, and our children. She says your love for Tommy helped her to understand sometimes you've got to get over yourself to be a good parent. She hopes to be one now." Caitlin beamed, tears forming in her eyes. "You are such a good guy." She took his hand.

"Seems those damn coins have worked yet another miracle, huh?"

"That's not the only little miracle that appears to have occurred," she whispered and she placed his hand on her ever so slightly protruding belly.

About the Authors

Christina St Clair, born and raised in England, has been a shop girl in London, an au-pair in Paris, a chemist in Pittsburgh, and is now a writer and pastor in the United States with several published novels that include supernatural fantasies and historical fiction. To learn more about her, visit http://www.amazon.com/Christina-St.Clair/e/B004WOR7EW/ref=ntt_dp_epwbk_0 She regularly posts on her blog: http://writeonweewriters.blogspot.com

Amanda Armstrong lives in England with her husband and daughter. This is her fourth fictional novel. For more information about Amanda's novels, visitwww.amandaarmstrong1974.co.uk or follow her on Twitter: @mandymia.

Also by Christina St. Clair
and Amanda Armstrong
at
Rogue Phoenix Press

Ten Yen True

Kaizen! That's what Caitlin, JJ, Paul, and Tommy need--to change for the better. When they each mysteriously receive one of four ten yen coins, none of them know or understand why or where their journey is about to take them.

Ten Yen True intertwines the lives of four people, all of whom have need of one another to bring about healing and wholeness and are being mysteriously helped by a Japanese monk. It is a story of hope, love, forgiveness and miracles, exploring the spiritual and psychological underpinnings of the main characters, demonstrating the interconnectedness of human beings.

By Christina St. Clair

Ten Yen

Amaya and Joumi meet, a few years after WW II has ended, at an American party in Tokyo. It's not easy to be a conquered Japanese citizen. Both have done things to survive that they regret. Joumi and Amaya immediately form a bond, but it is to be a stormy relationship with many inner demons to overcome if there is to be any hope of a lasting connection. The story incorporates accurate historical details about life in post-war Japan where people learn how to embrace defeat in ways that bring about love, community, and triumph. It is the prequel to Ten Yen True where a Buddhist monk brings healing to westerners he has never met.

By Amanda Armstrong

Ten Yen Forever

As an old monk comes to the end of his life, Amida bestows one final task upon him. Too weak to perform this himself, the monk enlists the help of his little apprentice, Akira, passing four miraculous ten yen coins on to him. Though confused and uncertain of what he must do, this task takes Akira across the Pacific to help those that need saving and those that didn't even know they needed saving. As dark forces threaten them, Holly, Paul and Tommy must once again trust in the miracle of the ten yen coins. This is the sequel to Ten Yen True where the monk brings healing to westerners he has never met

www.ingramcontent.com/pod-product-compliance
Lightning Source LLC
Chambersburg PA
CBHW050741230626
47052CB00004BA/903